POWDERSMOKE CANYON

Federal Judge Bates was looking forward to fishing with Tobacco Jones. First, he had to stop off in Muletown to finish the murder trial of Mary Helper. But there were people who wanted the trial stopped, and a masked killer had been hired to shoot down Bates before he arrived in town. When the wrong man was shot, Bates and Jones were left to face further gunsmoke in a frontier town flaming with violence.

Books by Lew Smith
in the Linford Western Library:

RAIDERS OF WHITE PINE

LEW SMITH

◆

POWDERSMOKE CANYON

Complete and Unabridged

LINFORD
Leicester

First published in the
United States of America

First Linford Edition
published July 1991

British Library CIP Data

Smith, Lew *1910 –*
  Powdersmoke Canyon. — Large print ed. —
  Linford western library
  I. Title
  813.52 [F]

  ISBN 0–7089–7036–2

Published by
F. A. Thorpe (Publishing) Ltd.
Anstey, Leicestershire

Set by Words & Graphics Ltd.
Anstey, Leicestershire
Printed and bound in Great Britain by
T. J. Press (Padstow) Ltd., Padstow, Cornwall

1

THE passenger train wound its way through the bottom of the canyon, black smoke spouting from the engine as it puffed and pulled the mixed train of three passenger cars and a carload of freight. On each side, high mountains rose upward, their rocky sides holding pine and spruce and fir trees. A fast-flowing mountain creek hurried downward on the south side of the right-of-way, and trout played in the still water behind the boulders that dotted the creek bed.

But to Judge Lemanuel Bates, the beauty of the mountains was an ordinary thing, and he slept the sleep of the just — a heavy-set man of about thirty, big body slumped in the velour seat.

However, the slim man sitting beside His Honor was not sleeping. He was lanky Tobacco Jones, and in ordinary

1

life he was the postmaster in Cowtrail, Wyoming. Now, out of sorts with the sunshine-filled world, Tobacco Jones chewed diligently on his cut of Horseshoe Chewing Tobacco, silently cursing the bouncing of the narrow-gauged train.

"Hard as ridin' a buckin' bronc," he muttered. "Joltin' along, drivin' a man's backbone up through the base of his skull. Wish I was out on Mule Crick a-fishin' them cut-throat trouts . . . "

A few miles ahead was Muletown. Judge Lem Bates and his partner had two good reasons for going into this Wyoming wilderness. One was to fish Mule Creek, for both had heard of the big trout to be found in that foam-tossed mountain stream, and both, at heart, were earnest fishermen. The other reason was quite different. His Honor had been summoned to sit on a change-of-venue trial. Both had welcomed the chance to leave Cowtrail for a while, for both hated routine. The train bounced over another rail section.

"Doggone train, Bates! Rough as a

hayrack — What the heck is the trouble now? Hang on, Bates, hang on!"

For suddenly, without a warning whistle, the train had jolted to a rough, rude stop. Brakes slapped down hard against brake wheels, and the cars almost piled up, they were stopped so hurriedly.

The impact, totally unexpected, snapped together Judge Lemanuel Bates' teeth, killing a snore half-born. The judge's neck jerked, his mouth flopped open again, and his eyes became round and startled as sleep fled.

"What the devil happened, Tobacco?"

"Danged hoghead of a engineer!" The postmaster, his equilibrium recovered, chewed Horseshoe with renewed vigor. "Prob'ly seen a sagehen on the track, or mebbe a grouse. If this dinky train hit anythin' as small as a pullet, it would be derailed, even if 'twere only goin' three miles per hour! What this country needs is — "

"A good five cent cigar," His Honor cut in, smiling at his partner's discomfiture. "Maybe we're already in Muletown."

"Muletown, Hades! We're miles from Muletown, Bates! You sound like a born optimeest, man. Look out that winder? Does the side of thet mountain look like the town of Muletown to you, Bates?"

Bates smiled, a big bluff man who took life's problems as they came. He looked out the window as he struggled to raise the pane of glass. But, like all railroad windows, the window jammed and stuck. He pushed upward, lips compressed, muscles bunched in coordinated effort.

They were in the canyon proper now, with steep walls on each side. Right below the right-of-way ran the noisy mountain creek, chuckling and dancing as it darted around rocks and boulders green with moss. Because of the proximity of the creek, huge boulders had been rolled along the edge of the grade; therefore the swirling waters could not cut into the grade and wash it away.

Judge Bates finally got the window open. He stuck his head outside. The mountain air, rushing down the canyon, was very chilly, even though it was

4

high summer. It came from off the snow-covered peaks with their eternal ice and glaciers.

"Maybe a landslide has slid across the track and stopped us," His Honor conjectured. "They do that a lot when a canyon has walls this steep. The ground gets soggy and — "

"No landslide!" Tobacco Jones spoke gruffly. "Prob'ly the ol' engine busted down. Limpin' along like a wind-busted hoss, it is. People should rise up against two things: high taxation and these bum railroads. Cinders in a man's eyes and mouth and in his grub — "

Suddenly the postmaster stopped talking. His mouth opened in surprise, and his pale eyes glistened as he stared at his partner, who had his head out the window.

"Bates — what was that I heard? A shot?"

Before His Honor could answer, the man across the aisle spoke. "Might have been a torpedo on the track. Didn't sound exactly like a shot to me. You and me are about the same build, Your Honor, but you sure are stronger than I am. You managed to open that window. I've been yankin' at my window for miles but can't get it to budge. Maybe I should get a crowbar, eh?" His wide face showed a good-natured smile at his own joke. "Bein' a salesman don't put no muscle in a man, I reckon. And I been a salesman for so many years I've forgot how many — "

The man stopped speaking. Again, from the front of the train, a shot had rung out — an ugly sharp sound that rudely punctured the calm stillness of the high mountain range. A bitter sound, sharp and mean, that was lost in the pines and spruce.

"That," said the salesman, "was a bullet, sure as shootin'. What do you see, Your Honor?"

Two cars ahead was the engine, puffing and panting, with steam shooting out around the piston. The conductor, who had hurried out to see what had caused the stop, had suddenly halted and for good reason, His Honor saw.

A masked man, carrying a sawed-off shotgun, had jammed the weapon against the conductor's ample belly, backing him unceremoniously against the baggage car. And the conductor, thinking of the damage that scattergun could do at that close range, had unceremoniously shot both pudgy hands upward, fingers trembling.

"Don't kill me — I got a wife and eight kids an my house ain't paid for an' — "

The judge said, "It's a holdup, men. Somebody has a gun on the conductor now!"

Tobacco Jones echoed, "A stickup, Bates? You sure, pal?"

"I got eyes, Tobacco, and I know a holdup when I see one. Nobody is stopping a train just to tickle the conductor's high ribs with a sawed-off shotgun! Somebody aims to rob this train!"

Hurriedly Tobacco Jones unbuckled his big watch from the gold chain, and

7

dropped the watch in his boot. "My ol' grandma done gave me that years ago," the skinny postmaster told the world in general. Then, on second thought, he loosed the gold chain, and it followed the watch in his boot. "Sure hope nobody tries to make me walk," he said.

Across the aisle, the fat face of the salesman was pale. Up ahead, a woman screamed, gurgled, then fainted. She was a beefy female, too, and she fell into the aisle. Her husband, a runt of a man, tried to get her up on the seat, and he kept appealing for help. Nobody helped him. Everybody had his or her own problems. The drummer gulped and tried to spit, but his throat was very dry.

Judge Bates, still looking out the window, allowed a puzzled scowl to mar the usual serenity of his wide face. He did not understand the holdup. For one thing, this was just a dinky old mixed passenger-and-freight train, and even if somebody did rob the mails, he wouldn't get anything of any value. Also, what few valuables and little money was carried by this handful of passengers was of small account.

With these points in mind, His Honor wondered why anybody would go to all the trouble to step outside the Law and rob this dinky train. He saw the engineer and fireman come down out of the cab with their hands held high. They moved over and joined the conductor, and the three of them stood in a row, hands over their heads, still under the awesome threat of the sawed-off shotgun.

The locomotive, resting now, had quieted somewhat, although its escaping steam still made a sibilant hiss that seemed to spit at the holdup men. Two men, both with faces masked, started back along the train, shotguns under their arms, boots pounding on the gravel.

Judge Bates heard a man say, "How'll I know this Judge Bates when I see him, Smitty?"

"Don't worry about that, Smitty. I'll know him when I see him, even though I ain't never seen him afore except in the newspapers. Fat gink, he is — heavy-set. We'll get him, Smitty."

"We shore will, Smitty."

Everybody was named Smitty, eh? Now the judge saw why the train had been stopped. This was no holdup! These men were out to kill a man — a judge! And that judge was nobody other than Judge Lemanuel Bates!

"Get your head back, fella!"

The words were snarled by one of the men. His shotgun blasted, but already Judge Bates had his head back. Beebees broke windows and tore into the wooden coach, but nobody inside was hurt.

Judge Bates said, "I got to get out of here, Tobacco. They aim to kill me. I heard them talking!"

"Kill you, Bates? Why? You're a stranger here — "

"I'm a judge, too, remember! Coming to sit on bench on a change-of-venue trial. Some people don't like judges."

"But why you?"

"Don't ask questions! I got to move . . . and move fast, friend! You coming with me, Tobacco?"

"Right on your boot heels, Lem!"

Their hands went out and grabbed their shotguns. Fingers locked around the trigger-guards. Both started for the back door of the coach. The fat salesman, scowling in puzzlement, looked at them in surprise.

"Where you two going?"

Neither partner answered. They were darting for the back door, shotguns upped pugnaciously. Somebody was in for a mess of trouble!

The salesman looked at his neighbor. "What in the heck is wrong with them two gents! Even if they got robbed, they wouldn't lose much, but if they get into a gunfight with these bandits, both might lose their lives!"

"Some men are funny," the neighbor gulped.

2

BATES and Jones halted in the vestibule, and here the sighing sounds made by the old locomotive were stronger, ringing out against the pines and dying against the rocky walls of the canyon. But His Honor had no ears for the panting of the old locomotive. His mind, ever agile and alert and sharp, was traveling ahead, building a pattern of attack.

"If we jump down on the right-of-way, Judge, they might start shootin' at us," Tobacco Jones said hurriedly. "Them two you saw on the ground ain't had time yet to come into the coach, and they'd shoot at us just as soon as we planted boots down on the ground, I'll bet!"

"Right, Tobacco, right."

Tobacco Jones spat hugely. "What is more, they might have a guard posted at

12

the back end of the coaches, too! They might also have a guard up on the side of the canyon."

"We have to chance those things," His Honor gritted. "We climb on top of the cars and gain altitude and from there — "

Already Judge Lemanuel Bates, in a very lumbering and anything but a judicial manner, was climbing the side of the car, heading for the top deck — a huge bear of a man, hands grabbing the iron ladder. And behind him, face wearing a determined scowl, came Tobacco Jones, shotgun in hand.

Once on top, His Honor planted his thick legs wide, his hand going down and grasping the free hand of his partner. Heaving and puffing, the jurist got the postmaster on top of the car, shotgun and all.

"You're limping, Tobacco."

"My watch. In my boot. Hurts my foot."

Despite the gravity of the moment, His Honor had to smile. "You won't travel far or fast with that hunk of gold in your justin," he allowed. "Keep your scattergun cocked, friend, and keep on the alert."

Tobacco said, "I'm ready."

"Shoot to kill. Make every shot, every beebee, count. These are ruthless men, stopping a train in broad daylight to kill a man — If the chance arises, kill them without a moment of compunction. Listen to the conversation in the coach, Tobacco."

They lay on the hot deck, the wooden boards warm under them, the sun pounding down with relentless energy. Heavy voices were making noises inside the coach. The sound, traveling upward, was clear in His Honor's ears.

"That's Bates over there, Smitty."

"Which gink you mean, Smitty?"

"Thet fat gink, of course! Thet one right ahead of us! Git ready to give him lead, Smitty!"

"I'm ready now, Smitty!"

Now the judge heard another voice — a pleading, terrified voice. The voice

14

of the fat salesman. "Men, for Gawd's sake, don't murder me. I ain't done nobody no wrong, I tell you. I'm only an innercent drummer a salesman — and I'm not — "

Boom!

The heavy, throaty roar of a twelve-gauge shotgun, barrel sawed off to give it more coverage, shook the coach.

Twice again the shotguns roared their spitting hot message of lead and death. A woman screamed, the sound high-pitched, terrible. Something hit the floor of the coach, and then the shotguns were silent.

"We got him, Smitty!"

"Good work, Smitty!"

"He won't sit on no trial, Smitty!"

"Let's make tracks outa here pronto!"

Judge Bates, face strained, face marked by anger and sorrow, stared at Tobacco Jones. The postmaster, for once, was not chewing — his long and horsy face was broken by tragedy, by the terror of what he and Judge Lemanuel Bates had heard in the car below them.

15

"Dirty two-bit killers! Killin' an innercent man, Bates!" The postmaster ground out his words with sullen anger. "We'll git them when they come out of that car — Bates, they don't want you in Muletown — that trial — Bates, you're in danger!"

Tobacco Jones halted. He had seen Judge Lem Bates angry before, but never had he seen such a terrible look in his partner's eyes.

"Those dirty, inhuman devils — they killed that fat, happy man. They thought he was me! Had I known that would have happened I'd've stayed in that car and fought them shotgun to shotgun — "

"Them women an' kids, Bates — they'da got kilt!"

Anger was still in His Honor's eyes — flat and ugly and demanding. Then this died before the bulldozer push of cold logic.

Tobacco Jones said quietly, "I can hear them backin' toward the door. Soon they'll step out onto the right-of-way. Shall we give them a chanct, Bates, or shall we just shoot them down like the c'yotes they are?"

"We shouldn't warn them . . . but we will. There comes one of them out now, shotgun in hand."

The bandit backed out of the car, shotgun cocked. They heard his boot find gravel. He stood there and ran a hard and determined glance along the sooty side of the old passenger coach to see if any heads protruded from windows. There evidently were no heads out, so he returned his attention to his killer-partner who was also backing out of the car.

"Coast clear, Smitty!"

The other killer, now on the right-of-way, said, "Well, we got that fat son, and now we had best make good our git-away, eh?"

Judge Bates, hunkered on the car, saw one of then, glance up at the brush on the side of the canyon, and he heard the man's voice clearly.

"Watch our backs, Smitty, from the bresh?"

"Sure thing, Smitty. Hey — " For the first time, evidently, the guard saw Judge Lemanuel Bates and Tobacco Jones on the car. "Hey, there are two hellions on top of the car, men!"

Then, without warning, the hidden guard fired, flame lancing out of a clump of willows on the opposite hill.

"Where at?"

"Top of the car — "

Judge Bates' deadly shotgun had already spoken. He could not see the ambusher but he could see a wisp of powdersmoke in the thick brush. He shot at this and his beebees landed.

He heard a terrified, pain-filled yell. Then the ambusher rolled out of the brush, Winchester sliding ahead of him. Limp and looking as if he were dead, the man rolled over the gun, caught his body around a boulder and lay there, quiet and out of the fight.

"You kilt one of the devils, Bates!" Tobacco Jones' voice, usually calm and smooth, boiled with savage ferocity. "His rifle ball hit the coach right ahead of your boots. Now git them two devils below us — "

Shotguns roared, spitting leaden death.

One of the killers had slid to a halt, automatically going to one knee the better to steady his shotgun. He shot hurriedly, but His Honor, shooting the moment before, had the advantage. But his lead did not hit the man squarely. Because of his speed, the judge had shot wide of his mark.

His beebees caught the man on the right side. They knocked the shotgun out of his grip. His second discharge plowed into the gravel and sand of the right-of-way. He was out of business and he wanted to get out of the territory . . . and he wanted to get out fast!

He fairly dived into the tall buckbrush. The brush hid him and he made his retreat under its protection. Judge Bates' shotgun, holding only two cartridges, was now empty. Hurriedly the jurist dug in his pocket for fresh shells. And now the scattergun of Tobacco Jones was yammering.

But the second killer, seeing the odds were too great after his partner had vamoosed, was tearing through the brush, making a hurried escape. Tobacco shot twice, emptying his shotgun. Then the roar was over, and in the distance could be heard the sound of hoofs heading out.

"I never had no luck at all," Tobacco Jones lamented, reloading his smoking shotgun. "You kinda got in my way, Bates, with that fat carcass of yours, so I had to wait until that gent got clear. Then he beats it into the bresh hell bent for election!"

"You might have stung him."

"I'm danged sure I never, Bates. But you plugged thet gent on the right side, 'cause you made him drop his scattergun sudden like. An' you kilt thet ambusher what was on the side of the hill plumb dead!"

Again hoofs roared, moving out into space. The engine sighed, somebody called to another person in the car, and the dead man lay in a heap, silent and

20

hearing nothing. The train crew came on the run, then. Passengers boiled out of the coach, some carrying short-guns.

Tobacco Jones asked, "What became of the gent what held the weapon on the train crew up at the front of the train?"

The conductor, panting from his run, answered with, "He drifted out without firin' a shot after you boys swung into action. There was four of them. Two went into the car, one held a gun on us, an' the other was the guard what you shot an' wounded."

A man had gone up the slope. He pushed the guard's body ahead of him, kicking him occasionally.

"Wounded, nothin' Conductor — this gent is plumb dead."

Tobacco Jones lamented, "An' we only kilt one of the skunks!"

"A skunk is a nice animal," His Honor corrected, his good humor coming back. "He burrows in the ground for roots and lives a nice life unless somebody decides to disturb him."

"Forgit it, Bates!" The postmaster

spoke surlily. "A man is dead inside that coach — a man they thought was you. He died because of you, Bates!"

Judge Lemanuel Bates' eyes showed pain. "And I am darned sorry for that, men and women." Then the look of pain died before one of cold resolve. "These killers will pay for this man's death."

"Amen to that," Tobacco Jones intoned.

3

THE dead man had worn a mask. Judge Bates' shotgun pellets, whamming in, had ripped the mask from his face when they had killed him. The beebees had also done something else: they made recognition of the man impossible. They had torn his face from his skull.

"Wonder who he is?" the judge asked.

"Nobody'll ever know who he is," the conductor said slowly. "His mug, gentlemen, is somethin' he used to own! Wonder if he has any identification? I can't go through his pockets, though, without the law to watch me."

"I'm the law," Judge Bates said.

A woman asked, "Then they killed that fat man in there — they thought he was you?" She was the woman who had screamed and then fainted.

"I'm Judge Bates."

The conductor said, "They must be somebody who don't want you to set on the bench in Muletown, eh?" He went on his knees and searched the man's pockets, emptying their contents on the ground. An old pocket-knife, a bandanna, a five-dollar gold piece and some silver change — but not a scrap of paper or anything pointing toward identification of the dead man.

"He rode on this raid prepared for death," His Honor said. "He has not a bit of identification."

The conductor tied all the stuff in the bandanna and spoke to the engineer and the fireman.

"Throw the stiff in the baggage car an' get your wheels rollin' for Muletown. Leave the prunehound lay where he fell until the sheriff can see him." The conductor looked suddenly at Tobacco Jones. "You limp, Jones. You git shot in the leg, fella?"

"My watch — it makes me limp."

The conductor regarded the postmaster with a sudden queer look. Plainly he doubted Tobacco Jones' sanity.

Judge Bates smiled. The crowd watched and listened.

"Are you in your right — How could your watch make you limp?" the conductor wanted to know.

"It's in my boot. I put it there afore the holdup started."

The woman who had fainted suddenly broke out laughing. A few men smiled, but for the most part they were a taciturn outfit, for death had taken one of their members.

The passengers climbed into the cars. The dead man was roughly thrown into the baggage coach, and there he lay sandwiched between a crate holding some chickens and a big box. The chickens cackled and raised a din.

"All aboard!"

Again the local passenger-and-freight ground on, heading for the end of the track, which was Muletown.

His Honor gloomily regarded the passing landscape through the fly-specked window. Soon they entered the outskirts of a little mountain town. First, they went past the town dump, the refuse of the town marring the beauty of a canyon. Then some unpainted houses came into view and the engine stopped in Muletown.

"End of the line, passengers. Muletown, last stop."

The train bucked to a stop, passengers lurching. Tobacco Jones had made an understatement when he had condemned this as the worst railroad line in Wyoming. Finally His Honor and Tobacco were on the platform, bags in hand. The judge had quite a job carrying three things: his bag, his whisky jug, and his shotgun, lovingly called Old Betsy.

"Nice-lookin' town, Jones."

Tobacco snorted around his chew. "Good for a lame dog to live in. Dirt an' filth. Like the poet said, 'Man marks the world with ruin.' Wonder where the hotel is in this dinky burg?"

Actually, the town looked better than their town of Cowtrail, but Judge Lemanuel Bates, realizing his partner's grumpiness, did not mention this fact. Muletown lay along the base of a timbered mountain, its main street — all two blocks of it — running north and south, parallel to the toe of the mountain. The buildings, some painted, some unpainted, were made of logs and sawed lumber. One, the biggest building in town, was made of native rock. Over this hung the Stars and Stripes, identifying it as the courthouse.

"Sure looks terrible," His Honor agreed.

Tobacco Jones sent his partner a sidewise look. Usually His Honor took the opposite side just for the sake of argument.

"Well, let's git a room an' shave an' wash up, Bates. I'll be an old man afore I can git all them cinders outa my whiskers."

Judge Lem Bates smiled. "Here's the sheriff's office, Tobacco. We had best inform him of this trouble we have encountered. We promised we would send him down to the depot, remember?"

"All right, Bates."

They were in front of the rock building. True to the judge's guess, it was the county courthouse. The door to the sheriff's office was open, and inside was a single desk. A long thin man, star buttoned to his open vest, sat in the chair, boots on his desk.

"Something, strangers?"

Judge Bates told him about the holdup. By that time the lawman's boots were on the floor and he was leaning forward, wide awake. Judge Bates talked, watching the long, ugly face for reactions to his words. The sheriff showed little emotion. His eyes just bugged out a little further as the judge stressed the fact that two men were dead down at the depot.

"Who are you two gents?"

"This is Tobacco Jones, postmaster of Cowtrail, Territory of Wyoming." The man's stupid indifference angered Judge Lemanuel Bates slightly. "And I, sir, am Judge Lemanuel Bates."

The homely face showed surprise, then went blank again. "I'm Sheriff Olaf Engstrand. Glad to meet you, Jones and

Bates. So you've come to set on Judge Weakspoon's bench for the remainder of the Helper trial, eh, Bates?"

His Honor studied the lawman coldly. Sheriff Olaf Engstrand, surprised by the coldness and hostility, asked feebly, "What did I say that was wrong, Bates?"

"Don't you ever use courtesy, Mr. Engstrand?"

The ugly face lighted. "Oh, pardon me a thousand times, Your Honor. I should have called you *Judge* Bates, eh? Danged sorry, 'kase I don't wanna git off on the wrong boot, Bates — I mean, Your Honor."

Judge Bates' wink was unnoticed by the blustering and fumbling sheriff, but Tobacco Jones winked back. The judge's plan was simple: he intended to put Sheriff Olaf Engstrand in his place at once and keep him there.

"Which is the best saloon in town, Sheriff Engstrand?" Bates asked.

"The Bucket of Suds. Ahead, down the street, this side. Owned by Mr. Bart Terry. You'll cotton to Bart. One of our leading citizens, Bart is. Reckon I'd best drag myself down to the depot, though. Why don't you two come along with me, and you can officiate, Your Honor, seeing you're the local judge now?"

"We'll go with you," His Honor said.

They left their suitcases in the sheriff's office. Down the street they went, lanky Tobacco Jones, face scowling, chewing tobacco as usual; gangling Sheriff Olaf Engstrand, also frowning; heavy-set Judge Lemanuel Bates.

They got the bodies out on the plank platform. Judge Bates watched them remove the bodies, watched Sheriff Olaf Engstrand search the pockets and bags of the murdered salesman.

"Wallet says his name is Henry Moore," the sheriff said in his high nasal voice. "Got a wife in St. Louis. I'll have to notify her. Be a hard shock to that good woman. This gent sold a combination of things, the evidence in this suitcase shows — corn and bunion remover, pain killer and elixir, and some other things, among them a salve for

30

removin' ringbone from a hoss's ankle. Reckon I'll try that salve on my ol' sorrel mare."

"Who is the dead bandit?" His Honor asked.

The sheriff gave him a quick penetrating look. "You don't expect me to identify a man what has his mug shot off, do you, Your Honor?"

"Thought you might know him by his build and his clothing."

The sheriff arose to his gangling height and regarded the man Bates had killed. He rubbed his bony hands together, knuckles crackling like chestnuts popping in a fire. He gave the dead man a long study, and then came to this glorious conclusion, "Lots of men around here with that general build he's got, an lots of them wear clothes like he does — levis, a flannel shirt. Did you look for his hoss?"

The conductor answered that. "We looked, Sheriff, but them bandits must've hazed him ahead of them, when they made their git-a-way."

"Not a bit of evidence in the world pointin' to his identity then," the sheriff said. "He'll be buried as a unidentified man. Another expense for the county. There'll be an inquest, of course. Cain't hol' it today, but the next time the train comes in, we'll hol' it pronto. Okay with you train men?"

It was. The train crew went downtown to eat, then to turn around on the Y, and head back down the mountain. His Honor and Tobacco Jones were just ready to leave the depot platform when, from behind them, came a harsh masculine voice.

"What's the matter here, Sheriff?"

The voice held an overbearing note, also a note of bluster and authority. For some reason His Honor did not like the surly tone of the man's voice. A glance at Tobacco Jones showed Judge Lem Bates that his partner was scowling.

While they had been talking with the train crew and the sheriff, two riders had ridden close to the platform. The whole town, of course, was at the depot, for it was not every day that the local train brought in two dead men, nor was it every day that the train was held up. Therefore the two riders had been unnoticed in the jabbering and confusion.

Sheriff Olaf Engstrand was all smiles, His Honor was quick to note. "Howdy, Bart Terry."

A heavy man, this Bart Terry. Weighing over two hundred, solid muscle and bone. A well dressed man, too. Blue suit, legs crammed into justin half-boots; his coat fitted his wide shoulders, and he packed two Colts — black butts protruding from black holsters affixed to a wide gunbelt that glistened with cartridges. But Terry's eyes, heavy and deliberate, were not on the sheriff; they rested momentarily on Judge Lemanuel Bates, appraising him, testing him, watching him. For a moment, their gazes met, and Bart Terry was the first to look away, his eyes moving over to Sheriff Olaf Engstrand.

Sheriff Engstrand said to the other

man, "Howdy, John Walker."

Walker also was watching Judge Bates. A thin man, this Walker, who could have been twenty-five, or forty-five. He wore California pants, also creased, and his boots were polished. His face was thin and dark with stubbled whiskers, his nose long, his mouth a hard, quick slash across his face. He also took his eyes from Judge Bates and put his gaze on the sheriff.

"Howdy, Sheriff," John Walker said.

Bart Terry's booming voice asked, "What happened here, sheriff?" He made the question a direct order.

Engstrand started his tedious explanation. Judge Bates and Tobacco Jones, standing to one side, were occasionally given sudden and quick glances by the two men. The judge considered the broncs ridden by the pair. He remembered the sheriff saying that the Bucket of Suds was the best saloon in Muletown, and that this saloon was owned by a gent named Bart Terry. Well, here was the owner of the Bucket of Suds, and here was a gent named John Walker riding with him. The judge, adding two and two and getting four, decided that John Walker was the right hand man of one Bart Terry.

Bart Terry had ridden his bronc hard. The bronc straddled by John Walker had also pounded a hot and heavy trail, His Honor decided. Terry's sorrel breathed heavily, flanks covered with white foam; the gray of John Walker also had foam on his shoulders, and a rope of foam hung from the part of the bit in the horse's mouth. But this was not what angered the jurist. What made him angry was the fact that Bart Terry's rowels had brought blood to the belly of his bronc. A tough rider had mistreated an innocent and faithful horse.

His tale ended, Sheriff Engstrand said, "Judge Bates and Tobacco Jones, these two men is Bart Terry an' John Walker. Terry owns the Bucket of Suds saloon, Your Honor."

"I shall pay him a visit soon," the judge said. "My jug needs replenishing,

Mr. Terry. Evidently you do not have the courtesy to treat your faithful horse with appropriate kindness for his good work under your saddle. Your spur rowels, sir, have torn into his hide."

Bart Terry had dismounted and was shaking hands with His Honor when the judge reprimanded him. Evidently he belonged to the school who liked to show physical prowess through a hard handshake. But, to Terry's surprise, the judge had a harder handshake than he, and Terry was glad to get his hand out of His Honor's grip.

The judge's words had put swift anger into Bart Terry's faded eyes. The anger passed, though, and when the saloonman spoke his voice was civil and obliging.

"I am indeed sorry about the horse, Your Honor. I put on the wrong spurs. Usually I use a star-rowel, but this time, for some reason, I got saw-roweled spurs on, by accident."

"An inhuman rowel," His Honor said.

Terry looked at Walker, who had not dismounted. "John, when we get home you file these rowels flat, savvy?"

"Sure." Walker spoke with cynical dryness. "Me, I'm a wonderful blacksmith — I couldn't weld two hunks of wet mud together with two sticks to push them."

The judge realized further words would be wasted, so he and Tobacco Jones took adieu of the group and headed for the sheriff's office to retrieve their suitcases.

Tobacco Jones said, "Wish I understood all I know about this deal, Bates. I'm up the crick, fella."

"We'll find out in time."

"Them two back there — thet Terry an' Walker — has rid them broncs hard. Wonder why?"

"I dunno. I know what you're thinking, though. They could have changed clothes somewhere and then ridden into town. As for that fellow I wounded, he wouldn't dare show up in town, unless he sneaked in to see the doctor. But this, partner, is all conjecture, and direct evidence stands up in court — even if it is a scattergun court, not a legal court of law."

They got their bags, the judge filled his jug at the Bucket of Suds, and they got a room at the Muletown Hotel, a two-story frame building. His Honor, tired from the swaying, jerking train, allowed himself the luxury of stretching out on the clean bed.

Tobacco Jones unpacked their suitcases, clucking like a mother hen as he hung up items of wearing apparel in the small clothes-closet. Sleep threatened to claim His Honor. He was just dozing off when Tobacco's sibilant whisper, laden with caution, came to his ears and jerked him wide awake.

"Somebody has sneaked up to the door, Bates. I heard their footsteps, silent like — "

"Tiptoe over and jerk it open, Tobacco!"

4

SILENTLY, walking on the balls of his feet, the postmaster went to the door, moving cat-like, his gaunt body slanting forward. And Judge Bates, shotgun in hand, lay on the bed, watching with vigilant eyes.

A horny hand went out, fastened its bony knuckles around the old doorknob. Outside, the judge heard the rustle of clothing; the shotgun came up slightly, and he swung his legs noiselessly over the edge of the bed. Then Tobacco Jones, moving with feline rapidity, jerked open the door.

The postmaster gasped, so great was his surprise. And Judge Bates, sitting there, shotgun ready, almost gasped himself, so startled was he. Then the shotgun lowered, and the judge said, "Something you want, miss?"

She was about twenty, His Honor

figured, and she was lovely, a beauty. A rangeland beauty, tanned by wind and sun. He saw blue eyes, a stubby nose, a mouth a shade too wide, but still a lovely mouth. A blue chambray shirt, bulging with feminine curves, and a pair of tub-faded levis.

She opened her mouth, but no words came. She colored prettily, and the judge said kindly, "Can we help you, miss?"

She did not give her name.

"Are you Judge Bates?"

She had a nice voice, slightly trembling now either from excitement or fear, or a combination of both.

"I am, miss. And this is my partner, Tobacco Jones."

Blue eyes darted to Tobacco, then back to His Honor. A tongue came out and wet pretty lips.

"I need help — Oh, forget it, please!"

Then she had turned and was running down the hallway. The judge hurried to the door, intending to catch her, but she was already out of sight. Evidently she had either darted out the rear door or had darted into a room. His Honor had caught sight of a nice back, and that was all.

"What in the heck, Tobacco?"

Tobacco Jones shrugged. "You got me, Bates. She wanted to tell us somethin', then got cold boots — an' turned an' run like a wounded doe."

"Wonder who she was?"

"Me, I dunno."

The judge's eyes grew soft. "She sure was a lovely little thing. Did you notice the way she filled that blue shirt?"

"Did you notice the way she filled them levis? She looked like somebody had melted her an' poured her into them. Wonder if a man ever gets so old he don't like to look at a purty woman's form, Bates?"

"If I ever get that old," His Honor spoke judiciously, "I want to die — die sudden and quick and on the spot. Again, though, what did she want, and who is she?"

Tobacco shut the door. "We'll find out who she is sooner or later. This is

41

a small jerkwater burg, Your Honor, an' unless I'm wrong, everybody here knows everybody else — and everybody knows everybody else's business, too."

"The curse of a small town, Tobacco. Well, I've had a brief rest, you've portered away our clothing, so let's mosey down on the street. Remember I came here to sit in Judge Weakspoon's place on the Helper trial, and I have not met the judge, and I know nothing about the case."

They went downstairs to the lobby. The ancient stairway creaked and groaned under their combined weights. The clerk was behind the desk. John Walker was looking at the register. That page had only two entries — the names of Judge Lemanuel Bates and Tobacco Jones, and their room number. Evidently Walker was interested in which particular room the partners had obtained from the clerk.

"Howdy, Judge Bates. Howdy, Mr. Jones."

The partners returned the salutation.

"Mr. Terry sent me over to make sure you two were comfortable," John Walker said, speaking in a silky tone of voice. "Mr. Terry is very public-spirited, working with officials to the best of his ability. It isn't often that Muletown gets such two well-known people to honor it."

The judge said dryly, "Did you file down those spur rowels yet?" He winked at Tobacco Jones.

John Walker said slowly, "Oh, yes, I have that yet to do." He turned and left, his back as stiff as a poker. Tobacco Jones grinned, and Judge Bates uncorked his jug. He put the jug on the counter.

"Have a nip, clerk?"

The clerk stared at the jug. His Adam's apple bobbed like a fishing cork in his rope-thin neck. He looked around, whispered, "The boss — No drinkin' on the job, much as I'd cotton to!"

"Go ahead."

The man wet his lips, raised the jug, and drank.

"Your Honor, you are a man after my heart, a gentleman of the first water. Is there something I can do for you?"

"Yes."

"Name it, sir."

"Who was that lovely young woman that came down the stairs ahead of us."

"That, sir, was Miss Imogene Carter."

"She sure wears nice pants," His Honor said.

The clerk's eyes showed surprise. "I beg your pardon, Your Honor! Well, that wasn't Imogene Carter — she wore a dress." The pale eyes narrowed in speculation. "For the life of me, I cannot remember a young woman with pants on going up the stairs, or coming down — and I've been behind this counter all the time."

"Your eyes, sir, must be bad. Good day, clerk."

They left the clerk blinking to test his eyes. Outside, Tobacco Jones said, "Well, we don't know yet who the gal was, Bates. But she never went past that clerk, 'cause he's got eyes like a gimlet. She snuck in the back door an' left thet way, too, I guess."

"Why?"

"I dunno, Bates."

They walked past the Bucket of Suds. From inside came the laughter of a drunken woman. Tobacco snorted in disgust. He shifted his chew to the other side of his cheek and said, "Thet gent John Walker — he was checkin' on what room we had. He weren't worried about our personal comforts, that gent."

"Another *why*, Tobacco."

Tobacco Jones spat hugely. "You got me, Bates. Him an' thet boss of his stink in my nostrils. They could have held up thet train an' then changed clothes an' rid into town."

"Why would they want to kill me?"

"Somethin' about this Helper trial, maybe. I wouldn't trust them two no further than I could heave a Hereford bull by the tail!"

"Those men, though, were named, *Smitty*, remember? All had the same name."

"Quit the joshin', Your Honor."

They were in front of the Mercantile

and under a sign that proclaimed, in black letters, that this store sold everything from a needle to a threshing machine. An old man, bent with age, was sweeping the already clean board walk.

"You two is Judge Bates an' Tobacco Jones, be ye not?"

"We are," His Honor said. "And you are who?"

"Henry is my name. Pardon me, Your Honor, but I shore hope you two clean up this mess here once and for always."

'What mess?"

"This Helper case."

His Honor asked, "Could you give me some information on it, sir, from the viewpoint of the common man, the taxpayer?"

"I sure can. I — "

From inside the store rang out a woman's voice. A harsh voice, heavy with authority.

"Henry, you come in this store right this minute — and keep your big mouth shut, hear me?"

"My wife," Henry said, and disappeared

into the store, broom over his shoulder. Tobacco Jones shrugged disgustedly.

"Marriage . . . An institution . . . An' a institution is also a house where they pen in crazy people . . . Bah."

"The mystery," declared Judge Lemanuel Bates, "is deepening, friend. What say we retrace our steps, until we reach the front door of the Terry emporium, The Bucket of Suds?"

"You just got a jug of likker. What else would you want in that den of iniquity?"

"You have forgot one item, Tobacco. By the admission of one John Walker, said Bart Terry is a community-minded man, a citizen who can impart the details of the so-called Helper case."

"He might, and he might not."

"You forget he is community-minded, working for the good of this sterling little mountain town!"

They went toward the Bucket of Suds. They were in front of that emporium when, without warning, a gun roared inside the saloon. It stopped the partners in their tracks.

"What the heck, Tobacco?"

The batwing doors broke open suddenly. First, they saw the man's rear come out; then the entire man, walking backwards, was backing toward them. He held a smoking gun in his fist.

"I want no more trouble," the gunman hollered into the saloon. "But if any of you want the roof raised, just tie into me, savvy! I'll give you a bellyful of hot lead, believe you me!"

The partners were directly behind the gunman who, as yet, had not heard them or seen them. They were directly in line of fire if somebody inside the saloon decided to call the gunman and shoot out the door at him.

"Get to one side, Tobacco!"

Tobacco Jones jumped like a jackrabbit scared out of the brush by a coyote. Judge Bates had never seen the lanky postmaster move so quickly. He himself was not slow, for he leaped to one side; already Tobacco was out of the range of fire. And the gunman, hearing them, fearing somebody would slug him from behind, turned and had his .45 on them.

He was a young man, slim and tall, and he wore a loose-fitting gray suit, the coat open, showing his brown gunbelt and his silk shirt and black string tie. Judge Bates, quick to size up an individual, read him as being about twenty-five years of age, and judged him to be rather intelligent, basing this assumption upon his clean-cut, handsome face.

"Who are you two men? You two gunmen working for Bart Terry?"

"I'm Judge Bates."

"Me, I'm Tobacco Jones."

The young man stared, moved to one side to be away from the door. His thin lips quivered with emotion. He lowered his gun as though the weight had suddenly become very, very heavy.

"I just killed a man in the saloon, Judge Bates. He drew his gun on me, and I claim the killing justifiable as self-protection. I therefore, Your Honor, deliver my gun, and my personage, into your custody for protection."

"And who, young man, are you?"

"My name, sir, is Weakspoon. Jack Weakspoon."

Judge Bates glanced sidewise at his partner. Tobacco Jones was scowling in puzzlement. The jurist pulled his gaze back to young Weakspoon. From inside the Bucket of Suds came the sounds of angry, raised voices, the scuffle of boots, the din of excitement.

"I came to sit on the local Bench in favor of a Judge named Weakspoon," His Honor said. "Could it be that you are related to that particular jurist, Mr. Weakspoon?"

"Yes, Judge Weakspoon was my father."

"*Was?*"

"Yes, he — "

Bart Terry, barging out the door of the Bucket of Suds, broke into the conversation with, "This gent — "

Terry said something else, too.

But Judge Bates was not looking at the saloon-keeper. Nor was he listening to Terry's words.

His attention was riveted on the area

where two buildings joined, across the street. The buildings were about three feet apart. A girl had darted out from between those two buildings.

For a moment she had stood there, poised and watching. A lovely young woman, blonde, and dressed in a man's shirt and a man's levi overalls. Then, without warning, she had ducked back again, darting swiftly — a scared fawn.

She became lost from view.

She was the girl who had knocked at the door, who had stuttered, and who had then bolted down the hotel hallway.

"Judge Bates, I say — "

The judge looked at the angry face of Bart Terry. "Who was that pretty girl?" he asked.

5

BART TERRY studied him momentarily.

"What pretty girl, Your Honor?"

"That one over by that building."

Terry looked. "That," he said, "is Miss
Imogene Carter."

The space between the buildings was
now empty. But in front of a store
across the street walked a young woman.
Imogene Carter was taller than the blonde
girl, and she was a few years older and
more sophisticated-looking. She did not
wear skin-tight levis, either. She wore
a pink hoop dress that gave her a
demure and very feminine appeal. The
judge saw leg-of-mutton sleeves and a
wide-brimmed hat that almost hid her
dark-skinned, pretty features. Her eyes
met those of the judge, and then Imogene
Carter demurely glanced to one side and
continued down the street.

"Not that woman," His Honor said. "That other one — the one with the pants."

"What other woman?" Bart Terry's eyes held a startled look. "There is only Miss Carter on the street."

"Mrs. Carter," a man corrected.

"A widow," another said. "Whether sod or grass, nobody cares."

Judge Bates looked at Tobacco Jones. "Did you see that blonde girl, Tobacco? She stood between those buildings for a while. The one that knocked on our hotel room door."

"Never noticed her, Bates."

His Honor gave up. Evidently everybody interested in the fight had concentrated his attention on Weakspoon, not on a stray woman. Some of the spectators were eyeing him with queer looks, His Honor was quick to note.

"I killed your gunman in self-defense, Terry."

Weakspoon spat out his words. His handsome face, twisted with anger, had in it also a touch of regret. "I hated to have to kill him, Terry, but he drove me to pulling my gun."

"For a shyster lawyer, Weakspoon, you're fast with your gun," Bart Terry grudgingly admitted. "Your Honor, come inside, and we'll give you details." He moved his big bulk to one side. "Weakspoon here killed my hired hand in cold blood, Judge Bates."

Weakspoon snarled, "You lie, you two bit saloon-keeper. When you call me a shyster lawyer, make room for a fight, fellow! I might be a lawyer, but that doesn't make me a shyster, savvy?" His eyes were cold and his face was not handsome now — it was twisted with rage, the lips drawn back, the eyes cold fire. "I shot in self-defense, and I can prove it in court."

"You lie again!"

Weakspoon started for Bart Terry, fists raised. But Tobacco Jones, moving in rapidly, pinned the attorney's arms at his side, hanging onto the lawyer. And Judge Bates, never one to tolerate fisticuffs, moved his bulk between the two men, his voice raised in conciliatory tones.

"Now, now, men — Keep calm, at all costs. Hot heads never solved any deep problems yet — Terry, put down your fists!"

Terry said, "He insulted me, an' by Gawd — "

"I'll put you under arrest," His Honor threatened. Terry's face was dark with thunder. Then discretion came in, blowing the clouds away, and his face turned sunny. He stepped back into his saloon with, "As you say, Your Honor. I'm obliging and will work with the law to the utmost of my ability — "

"Weakspoon, act like a man, not a hot-headed youth, please."

Weakspoon said to Tobacco Jones, "Turn me loose, Mr. Jones. You have my promise."

Tobacco released the barrister. By this time Sheriff Olaf Engstrand was at the scene, his long horsy face registering surprise.

"What's the matter, Judge Bates?"

The Judge picked up his jug. He had

dropped it in the melee. Carefully he inspected the crockery. Tobacco Jones, pushing Lawyer Weakspoon ahead of him, entered the saloon. Still the judge looked carefully at the jug.

"Cracked?" Engstrand asked.

"No." The judge looked at the sheriff. "Lawyer Weakspoon backed out of the saloon, gun in hand. There has been a shooting inside. Let's go in."

"Who shot who?"

"Weakspoon allegedly shot somebody, but I don't know who."

"Our job is inside," Engstrand said importantly. "I was a-fixin' to ride out to that holdup scene and look for clues, but this is more pressin' business."

They went inside the Bucket of Suds. Bart Terry, his broad face wearing a cynical smile, stood beside the bar. When Lawyer Weakspoon walked by the saloon-man, Terry swung hard with a right fist. The fist, launching upward, hit the unsuspecting Weakspoon flush on the jaw.

Weakspoon went backwards. His arms

flailed like a Dutch windmill caught in a cyclone. He tried to grab a hand-hold on the air but the air was not cooperative. The lawyer crashed into the bar back first, swayed over the rail and then sat down, stunned but not out.

Judge Bates shook his head in feigned disgust. "And you, Mr. Terry, gave me your word you would be a good man, and here you break your word by slugging this unfortunate barrister — "

"Unfortunate! He's lucky I ain't killed him!"

The judge put on a cloak of supreme sadness. The world seemed sour, for a man had broken his word.

"Go over to Weakspoon, Terry, and help him to his feet, and then apologize."

Terry took a long look at the jurist. "Judge Bates, with all due respect to your personage and office, are you in your right mind?" He did not wait for an answer. "I'll go over and visit him and kick the stuffin' outa him — "

He started for Weakspoon, who was dazedly trying to get to his feet. For the moment, Terry had his back to Judge Bates.

The Judge's words had worked their purpose and the judge had Terry in the right position. His heavy whisky jug glistened as it rose and came down. Terry did not move another inch forward. The jug made a harsh sound against Terry's skull. Terry made another sound as he hit the floor. Then he was lying unconscious at Lawyer Weakspoon's feet.

"Holy smoke," Weakspoon said shakily. "Thanks, Judge Bates, thanks. He almost knocked me cold."

"He's cold himself," Tobacco Jones said, grinning. Judge Bates spoke to the bartender, who still had his mouth open. "Close your mouth, friend, because you attract flies." The jaw clipped shut with loud agility. "When your boss comes to, bartender, tell him what happened to him."

"For you, Your Honor, I will do that . . . with pleasure."

"Well spoken, sir."

Judge Bates was smiling. His broad

face appeared very jovial. And Tobacco Jones, who was biting off a fresh chew of Horseshoe, also grinned. With one blow, His Honor had established his supremacy over Bart Terry.

"And now, gentlemen, where is the dead man?"

That question was not answered just then. For a man barged through the crowd — a thin man with a hard dark face. And then John Walker stopped, hands hooked in his gunbelt, and stared down at Bart Terry. "What happened to Bart?"

"I knocked him cold," Judge Bates said, neglecting to mention he had slugged Terry with his jug not his fists.

John Walker looked at His Honor. At first Walker's slate-colored eyes held doubt; then this doubt gave way to certainty.

"Your Honor, you are tougher than I thought."

"Tie into me some time," Judge Bates invited him coldly.

Walker flushed with anger, then

subsided. He went to one knee beside his unconscious boss. Sheriff Engstrand said, "Maybe I'll have to arrest you, Judge Bates." He said it in a very uncomfortable tone of voice. "For disturbin' the peace, the warrant would read."

"You forget one thing, Sheriff."

"Yeah, an' what is that one thing?"

"I'd have to sign the warrant. And I sign no warrants calling for my *own* arrest, you may be assured of that."

"By gosh, that's right."

Judge Bates was getting hot under the collar. Here he had come to Muletown to sit on the local Bench and do some fishing in Mule Creek. They had shot at him, held up the train, killed an innocent salesman, and he, in turn, had killed an unidentified bandit. Then a girl in levis kept pestering him, not to mention the fact that so far he had found out nothing about the case over which he was to preside. Lawyer Weakspoon had used the verb *was* when mentioning his father, which seemed to indicate that Judge Weakspoon was deceased.

"Where is this dead man?" he demanded.

The bartender hurriedly said, "His carcass is over beyond that overturned card table, Your Honor."

"Thanks."

Jug in hand, His Honor moved forward, half the town of Muletown on his heels. The dead man was not a lovely sight. For one thing, Lawyer Weakspoon had used a soft-nosed .45 slug, and it had scooped out most of the man's face. At this moment, Weakspoon staggered over and slumped in a chair, holding his aching jaw.

"Wonder if I have any teeth left?" the lawyer asked the world in general. "Judge Bates, will you look into my mouth, please?"

"I'm no dentist." His Honor was still gruff and angry. "I only look into the mouths of horses and jackasses, not humans. You lawyers never run out of wind. As long as you can shoot off your mouths, you're successes. Who is this dead stiff, men?"

"One of Bart Terry's cowpunchers," a man said.

Judge Bates sent a glance toward the speaker. He was a man of about fifty years of age, short and pot-bellied, wearing a well-tailored suit. Plainly he was a city man and, just as plainly, he was out of place in this cow town.

"Did you see the shooting, sir?"

"I did."

"Who drew first, sir?"

"This dead gent. The lawyer shot second. Only thing was, this dead gent pulled too fast, and he missed."

"There'll be a coroner's jury over this shooting," His Honor said. "You be there. What's your name?"

"Mike Jacobs."

"What's your business?"

"My business, if you will pardon me, Your Honor, is my own affair, and none of yours."

"Well said, Mr. Jacobs."

By this time, John Walker had Bart Terry on his feet, although Terry's feet were uncertain. His knees wanted to spring out of line and dump his carcass back onto the floor. Terry braced himself against the bar and shook his head slowly. But this evidently hurt too much, so he stopped and stared dully at John Walker.

"What the blazes happened to me, John?"

"Judge Bates slugged you."

Memory flooded Terry's eyes. "Oh, yeah, I had just knocked down the lawyer. What did he hit me with?"

"His jug."

Judge Bates watched Terry, wondering if the anger in the man would overcome his better judgment. But when Terry looked at him the ghost of a smile hovered over his hard lips.

"I'm sorry, Your Honor. I lost my head." He studied Mike Jacobs. "You lie, fella! My man drew last, I say!"

"That," said the judge, "will be for the jury to decide. Now why did this gunman of yours tie into Weakspoon?"

"I dunno."

Weakspoon said hotly, "You do know,

63

Terry. You want me out of the way. You got him to pull against me in hopes he could kill me!"

"You lie."

This conversation, His Honor noticed, was getting exactly nowhere.

The judge spoke to Sheriff Olaf Engstrand. "I order you to jail Lawyer Weakspoon, Sheriff."

Weakspoon stared. "On what charge?"

"Murder."

"He drew first."

The judge again spoke to Engstrand, this time in a quieter tone of voice. "Take him to the lockup and make it pronto."

"But I ain't got no warrant."

Judge Bates moved closer to Engstrand, who hurriedly stepped back while Tobacco Jones grinned. The sheriff had been quick to notice the particular way the judge held onto his jug. One wicked swing of the jug and Engstrand could get what Bart Terry suffered.

"He goes to jail, Your Honor."

"I shot in self-defense and I claim — "

The rest of the words were cut off when Engstrand throttled the lawyer. The sheriff's bony fingers twisted the man's collar down until the lawyer could barely squeal. Then, pushing the lawyer ahead of him, Engstrand left the saloon, a man puffed with importance.

Judge Bates took a drink. Then he wiped his mouth and looked at John Walker.

"You looking for trouble, Walker?"

"No, but if any comes my way — "

Their eyes met, held.

Anger held sway in Walker, driving savage glints into his eyes.

Bart Terry said, "No trouble, John."

Walker said, "All right." He turned and went to the back of the saloon and entered a door marked: PRIVATE. The door went shut hard, the report loud.

"You rubbed his fur the wrong way, Your Honor," Bart Terry said.

Judge Bates spoke dryly. "Maybe I did," he said.

"You didn't come into town to boss this town," Terry said, almost too quietly.

"You came into town to sit on Judge's Weakspoon's bench in the Ree Helper trial, remember?"

"You threatening me, sir?"

Bart Terry shook his head. "Just reminding you," he said.

"My memory is good," Judge Bates declared.

Tobacco Jones, reading all the symptoms of another fight, tugged at his partner's sleeve.

"Let's make tracks outa here, Judge," he said.

The judge nodded.

6

OUT on the plank sidewalk, the judge stopped, staring at the space between the two buildings. "Hold my jug, quick! There she is again — running away!"

"What the heck is wrong with you, Bates?"

But His Honor, in a very unjudicial manner, was running across the street, speeding as fast as his legs would carry him.

Tobacco followed at a trot, seeing no reason to run through the heat. By this time, His Honor was in the alley. Here was confusion and debris and flies — garbage cans loaded to the brim, lids aslant, with flies swarming. Trash barrels, black with soot, also littered the alleyway. There was a barn at the end of the alley, and the judge was a pace behind the girl as she darted into the gloomy interior.

"Stop!"

But she got on a horse that was back of the barn — and the bronc, starting out on a wild run, did nothing but kick back sand into Lemanuel Bates' wide face.

He stopped, grinning. She *was* a wildcat, no two ways about that!

"What the Hades is wrong with you, Bates?"

"I," Bates told Tobacco Jones, "have been out chasing a woman, friend. Let's find out something about her, eh?"

"Somebody will know her."

They went out on Muletown's main street. The old man was again sweeping the sidewalk in front of the store. Judge Bates asked him some questions and the storekeeper studied him with what seemed surprise.

"You mean that gal thet jes' rid a hoss by here — hell for leather — ? You wanna know who she is, Your Honor?"

"Is there anything odd in my request, Henry?"

The old gums showed in a toothless

grin. "I'll tell the world there is, Judge Bates. 'Cause you see, man, it's this way — you come into town to prosecute that gal, to sit at her trial."

"I did?" Judge bates smiled to cover his surprise. "Who is the girl, and what is her handle?"

"That's Ree Helper."

Judge Bates looked toward Tobacco Jones, who chewed with slow rhythm. "What is the charge, sir, against Miss Helper?"

"Murder."

"Whom did she murder?"

The old man stared, leaning on his broom. "You mean you don't know who she kilt?" He seemed overcome with surprise. "Why, she kilt — "

"Henerry, come in here, and shut your big mouth!" Again, that loud feminine voice, thick with authority. "You learn to keep yore big mouth shut, Henerry, and come in here without another word said, understand!"

"Comin', Emma."

"Make it snappy, Big Mouth."

Henry shuffled around, heading for the door. "Danged ol' woman — been hooked to her for nigh onto fifty years — a half-century of misery — " He shot a quick look at Judge Bates, then disappeared into the store.

The door slammed, and Henry was gone.

The judge pivoted, anger scrawled across his wide face. His eyes were hard beads.

"Where to?" Tobacco Jones asked.

"To Engstrand's office."

They stalked down the street, the judge now toting his jug, his shotgun under his arm. He had the air and the stride of a determined man. Tobacco Jones, long legs working, kept stride, burdened only by his scattergun. They swung into Sheriff Olaf Engstrand's office, surprising the sheriff and Lawyer Weakspoon, who were conversing.

"I want some information, gentlemen."

Sheriff Olaf Engstrand was very courteous. He unlimbered and arose to his gaunt height, homely face beaming.

"Be seated, gentlemen. I was discussing something with Mr. Weakspoon before putting him behind bars."

Judge Bates remained standing. Tobacco Jones sank into a nearby chair. The judge looked at one man, then the other.

"I'll get to the point," he told them. "I'm here to sit on the local bench in a change-of-venue trial. I only know what the attorney general told me, and he told me to go to this town and preside at this trial."

"Sometimes he is very sparse on details," young Weakspoon said, watching the judge. "Maybe I could help you, Your Honor?"

"Your father, Judge Weakspoon, is dead, I understand?"

"Murdered, sir."

"And who is the alleged murderer?"

"A woman, sir. In fact, not a woman — a young girl."

Judge Bates nodded. "And what is her name, gentlemen?"

Again Lawyer Weakspoon answered.

"Her name is Mary Helper, commonly called Ree Helper."

"She is blonde, lovely, and about twenty or so?"

Weakspoon nodded. "Have you met her, Your Honor?"

"No, but I've heard about her. Continue, Lawyer Weakspoon, please."

"My opinions, sir, might be biased, for the dead judge was my father, and blood is thicker than water."

"Go on with your story."

"Ree Helper and her father lived out in Thunder Canyon, which is east of here a few miles. Her father, it seems, was mysteriously killed. One of her neighbors was out looking for some stray cattle and was searching the country with his field glasses. He saw the girl digging a grave."

"Yes, go on."

"She buried her father in that grave. The neighbor rode into town and reported the news to my father."

"Why didn't he report it to Sheriff Engstrand?"

Engstrand said, "I was out of town that day. Bart Terry claimed somebody was rustlin' some of his cattle and I had rid out to investigate. Bart owns a big ranch, too, you know — Bart is very influential, Your Honor, and swings a number of votes — "

"You've said that before. So Miss Ree reported this to your father, Mr. Weakspoon?"

"That she did, Judge Bates. Kirby Helper, her father, was once accused of rustling Bart Terry's cattle, but that is neither here nor there. My father, of course, held an inquest, and Ree testified that her father had been mysteriously shot, and had died from ambush wounds."

Tobacco Jones chewed thoughtfully. Sheriff Engstrand leaned forward in his swivel chair and cracked his knuckles with loud rapidity. Judge Bates wished the man would stop but he said nothing as he watched Lawyer Weakspoon, who seemed hesitant about going further with the conversation.

"Continue, sir?"

"Evidence was introduced showing that she and her father often quarreled violently and at some length. Some claimed she had killed her father in a fit of rage. She was indicted for murder. She was arrested and incarcerated. Then, at her trial, she broke loose and fled."

"She got away from one of my deputies," Engstrand said in defense. "I fired the gink right off the bat. Don't want men like him on the public payroll."

Judge Bates nodded, eyes thoughtful. "Then what?"

"Well, she took to the brush, and they tried to run her out — but they couldn't. My father said he would ride out alone and see her. He did this, and then we found his body. He was shot from behind — through the back — "

Judge Bates nodded. Things were clear now. "How long ago since your father got ambushed?"

"About two weeks. The attorney general then sent for you. Frankly, Your Honor, the attorney general paid you a great compliment by giving you this case. As

74

he told me in a letter, he figured you were the only legal mind in the Territory who could and would bring about justice in this case."

"Do you think Miss Ree Helper murdered her father and then ambushed your father, sir?"

"I do not wish to render an opinion. I am, as you know, county attorney. Or did you know that, sir?"

"Your job, then, is to prosecute her. Where is she now?"

"We can't catch her," the lawyer said.

Sheriff Olaf Engstrand said, "I've plumb wore myself an' my deputies out tryin' to catch her. She rides the fastest broncs they is and she knows that kentry like I'm supposed to know the back of my hand." He regarded the back of his right hand with curiosity. "That's a crazy sayin', men. I dunno what the back of my hand really looks like." He got to his feet. "Me, I got to git out to the scene of thet robbery. Got a deputy out there waitin' for me." He looked at Judge Bates. "Do I have to jug my ol' friend here, my pal Lawyer Weakspoon?"

"Get on your way," His Honor ordered.

Engstrand speared a Winchester rifle from the deer-horn gunrack and went outside with chiming spurs.

"What were the Helpers doing out in Thunder Canyon?" the judge asked.

Weakspoon said, "They took up a homestead out there."

"And they settled on land claimed by Bart Terry, eh?"

"Yes, he used to run cattle in Thunder Canyon."

Suddenly Judge Bates asked, "Do you think Miss Helper murdered your father? From what you imply, your father had much influence over her, even talking her into coming into town for an inquest when her father was killed though she knew evidence pointed toward her."

"My father was a good man. He had no enemies."

Judge Bates smiled at that. "Very much in error, sir. Any judge, regardless of his personality, has many, many enemies. Every day he makes enemies in his court, even though he administers unbiased justice. Well, you go back to a cell, Lawyer Weakspoon."

The lawyer studied him. "Are you joking?"

"I got the cell keys," Tobacco said, taking them off a hook on the wall.

Judge Bates had him by the collar, lifting him out of the chair. "I never joke about serious matters, sir. Into a cell you go."

They took the lawyer down the tier and Tobacco unlocked a door. Judge Bates unceremoniously pushed the barrister inside, and Tobacco Jones, grinning widely, slammed shut the door, then shook it to see that it was securely latched. Weakspoon sat on the bunk and glared at them.

"I could get you for false arrest!"

"You killed a man, remember."

"Only one of Bart Terry's gunmen. Bart sicked him on me. Bart wants me out of the way."

"Why?"

The lawyer hesitated. His eyes measured

those of Judge Bates and he wet his lips.

"Forget it," he snarled.

With Tobacco Jones in the lead, the partners left the jail, went into the office, and stepped outside. Dusk was beginning to come in on silent feet and was encroaching upon the rangelands.

They stopped in front of a log building. A sign, dull with faded letters, hung over the door.

DR. HENRY GOODENOUGH, M.D.

The door opened to a turn of the knob, but Dr. Henry Goodenough was not in the office. Judge Bates was in a room that needed the floor swept and the windows washed. The medico's desk was covered with papers and bottles. One bottle held a note that said:

I'll be back when I get good and ready to come back.

Dr. Henry Goodenough.

Tobacco chewed, asked, "What suddenly

78

made you come into this doc's office, Bates? You ain't sick, be you?"

"My health," replied Judge Lemanuel Bates, "is in very excellent shape. But back yonder along the railroad track I filled a bandit full of beebees, remember? That man might have sought medical attention. If such is the case, then the doctor will know the identity of that bandit and this case can be solved."

"But the doc ain't here."

Judge Bates again read the note. "Sounds like a salty ol' rooster, Jones. Might be good company to know. Wonder where he is?"

They made a few inquiries.

"Doc left town just a few hours ago," one man said.

Another said, "He went over to Rawhide to spend a month with his daughter there. He's only got the one daughter, you know — "

"He ain't in Rawhide," another declared. "He's over to Horseshoe, doctorin' that merchant over there — "

Bart Terry and John Walker stood

in front of the Bucket of Suds. Terry regarded them with a steady look that held no emotion, but John Walker's eyes held a flare of sullen dislike.

"Doc left town for a month or so," Terry said. "Told me he was going on a vacation. Be you sick, Your Honor?"

"Belly cramps."

Terry nodded. "Maybe that railroad ride did you no good. Rough track, like ridin' a bronc, an' it can jar a man's innards terrible."

"They need a new railroad into here."

"That they do, Your Honor."

The partners ate at a café called The Broken Spur.

The waitress was very pretty — small, not over five feet, and dark-haired. Judge Bates winked at her. She brazenly winked back, laughed, tossed her head.

"I've heard about you, Judge Bates. For a young man you sure are widely known around the Territory. And they say you are single, too."

"I sure am, young lady."

"Lou is my name. I'm single, too."

"We oughta get married," the judge said. "We'd make a fine-looking couple, Lou."

She laughed — a tinkling, bell-like sound. "I'm particular," she said, serving their meal.

Judge Bates joked with her. Tobacco Jones ate in dour silence. They paid and went to their hotel room. Tobacco dozed on the bed, boots off, while His Honor read the old newspaper found on the dresser. Finally Judge Bates threw the paper into the wastepaper basket.

"Tomorrow, Tobacco, we'll have a long talk with Miss Ree Helper."

Tobacco Jones studied him momentarily. "Sure, we'll have a talk with her — if we can catch her, the antelope!"

Judge Bates stood up. "We'll have to catch her, Jones. I don't want to go to bed yet. Lou said the Cheyenne stage would bring in the new papers, and I'm going down to her café and get a paper."

"You sure you don't want to see her, and aren't using the newspaper for an excuse?"

Judge Bates smiled. He went down the

81

creaking stairs and came into the lobby, where he nodded to the old clerk, and then he stepped out into the darkened night. To reach Lou's café, he had to go through an alley. He was in this alley when he saw the man and woman. Neither of them saw him, and shamelessly he watched them.

He could see them clearly enough to identify them. The man, he saw, was Bart Terry. The woman was rather short, and at first he thought she was Lou; then he realized the waitress was even shorter than this girl.

Bart Terry kissed the woman long and lovingly, and the woman kissed him back.

He sneaked around them, going around a building. He was a little surprised, for the woman had been Ree Helper.

He walked in the shadow of a building. Too late, he heard boots behind him. They came fast, making a scuffling sound in the dust, and Judge Bates turned — a big man, cat-fast on his feet. But despite his speed, he was still too slow.

He saw a dim, shadowy form, saw the uplifted club. He ducked, but did not duck soon enough, and the club came down without giving him time to identify the man who wielded it.

And then, with a loud bang, the world went dark.

the safe a fine, shadowy form, saw
the wilted club he clutched, but did
not think how crude, and the club
came down, catching him full on the
bony forehead, who wielded it

7

LONG fingers crammed brass-
rimmed cartridges into the loops
of the oiled cartridge belt. Lamplight glistened on the cartridges with
metallic certainty. Lamplight reflected
from the polished black butt of the
big Colts .45 that lay on the table.
The flickering lamplight went upward,
showing the tight and bestial face of the
gunman, John Walker.

"Well, I knocked him cold as a stone,
boss."

"Where is he?"

"Layin' out there in the alley where
I slugged him."

"He have his jug with him?"

John Walker chuckled; the sound was
dry and without mirth. "He sure did
have, Bart. Tried to slug me with it,
but I used a club — and I hit too fast.

Then I uncorked his jug and poured some whiskey over him to make him smell good an' strong. Then, by gosh, I tipped the judge's jug meself, and had a long drink on the old boy."

"He recognize you?"

Bart Terry studied his gunman carefully. The lamplight glistened from his eyes, slanting and wicked and mean.

"I wore a mask, Bart. Tied my bandanna cross my jaws-sides, it was dark in the alley. Where you been, anyway?"

"Out courtin' Ree Helper."

John Walker allowed his thin lips to show a tight smile. "You have any luck, Romeo?"

Bart Terry paced the floor. Three steps one way, three back; he locked his hands behind his back and threw his head up and did some thinking. And John Walker, watching his boss, was silent, busy with his own thoughts.

Bart Terry smiled, but with his lips only — his eyes were deadpan and ugly as usual. "I hugged her and played up to her. I'll work her into signin' over that deed yet, so help me I will."

"I doubt it."

Terry stopped, regarded his gunman. Walker licked a cigaret into shape, tongue red against the wheat-straw paper, his thin fingers twisting paper and Bull Durham into a hard cylinder.

"You doubt too much," Terry growled.

John Walker's hands trembled slightly as he lit his cigaret. This egotistic man sometimes irritated him, but Walker knew his place in this, and that place was secure. When this was over, he would be worth money. And it was money he wanted. Just as Bart Terry wanted money — lots of money.

"Forget it," Walker said easily.

Bart Terry paced the floor again, boots grinding on the flooring. They were in Terry's office in the rear of the Bucket of Suds Saloon. Through the door seeped the sounds of men and women out in the saloon. A fiddle squeaked, the sound thin.

Bart Terry seemed to be talking to himself. "We bungled things, Walker.

First we killed that drummer, thinkin' he was Judge Bates. How was we to know that Bates and Jones had climbed on top of that car? How was we to guess that the fat drummer was not Bates? The same description fitted both of them!"

"Good luck our gunman got his face shot off. That sure was a stroke in our favor. 'Cause if his mug hadn't got blasted off by Bates' scattergun, they could have identified him as workin' on your payroll, Bart."

Bart Terry stopped, head down in thought. He beat a fist against a palm and said, "We had some good luck there, that's right. But we had bad luck when Joe got winged by Bates. What about Doc Goodenough, Walker? He's out to the ranch treatin' Joe, and if Goodenough talks everybody will know we engineered that holdup."

"How will they?"

"Goodenough will tell about Joe bein' filled with beebees. That'll make everybody think of a shotgun, and then they'll remember that holdup."

Walker blew smoke, the smoke thin and gray around his handsome face. His nostrils quivered as he puffed again.

"Doc won't talk, Bart. I'll have a heart-to-heart confab with him, out to the ranch, and I'll point out various points to him. Then if he thinks about talking, I still have my .45. I'll impress him that way, Bart."

"He's not one to swallow a threat, even if he is an old drunk. Bates wanted to contact him to see if he had treated a wounded man, too. Bates and Jones are nobody's fools."

"Maybe I should go out in the alley with the Winchester that has a silencer and I should kill Bates before he comes to, Bart."

"Might be a good idea."

John Walker crossed the room, took the Winchester from the rack, and dug in a drawer for the silencer. Then Bart Terry's words stopped him and he closed the drawer, leaving the silencer inside.

"No, we won't kill him. Bates is nobody's fool, and he might take the hint and run out on us, scared to the gills. Then that man of ours had to miss gettin' that shyster lawyer. We sick him against the lawyer, aiming for him to get the lawyer out of the way because he knows too much — and by Gawd, the lawyer kills our gunman! This ain't been a good day for us John."

"Never knew Weakspoon could handle a gun that fast. Well, he's in jail now, and I could slip down there and shoot him behind the bars, Bart."

Walker's eyes glistened wolfishly. He wet his lips, his tongue darting out snake-fast, wet and red.

Bart Terry paced, hands locked. Finally he said, "No, we don't do that. Signs would point to us, seeing the shyster was gunned by one of our hands. People would claim we killed him to avenge the death of our gunman, and we got to keep public opinion away from us, John."

"Bates is suspicious of us."

"What makes you say that, John?"

Walker chose his words with extreme care. "He's no stupid ass, Bart. Judge

Weakspoon got murdered, and Judge Bates knows he might get killed, too. I was lucky I got behind him to slug him. Even at that, he heard me. He's like a big cat, that man — fast on his feet — "

"We got to get rid of Weakspoon," Bart Terry finally said. "He's a double-crosser, that son. He sold his own father down the river, even if you was the gent what ambushed Judge Weakspoon — "

John Walker's voice was angry. "For Gawd's sake, Bart, go easy on that talk, savvy!" Anger had pulled his thin face into hard set lines. His eyes were narrowed slits, his hands poised over his guns. "The walls might have ears. And I don't want to hang because of your big mouth. This shyster don't know I ambushed his father — only you an' me know that. So keep it between ourselves, savvy? If you don't I'll — "

"What'll you do, John?" A soft, whispering voice, laden with danger. "You ever make a move to lift a gun against me and I'll show you some gun speed. Don't threaten me, unless you want to reach."

They stood like that, poised and ready, hands over guns. Taloned hands, trembling hands, hands ready to swoop down, grab gun-grips, slide .45s upward, the steel moving against the oiled leather holsters. In this moment, each found what he had long suspected — they hated each other. But greed was stronger even than hate, and John Walker drew his hands back, his lips laboriously creating what he hoped was a smile. "You're the boss, Bart."

Terry drew back his hand, and his voice assumed an oily smoothness. "We gotta work together, John, cause we're both in this to our necks. Don't forget that I was the one that shot Helper, fella."

"Even up, Bart. One for each of us. All right, what is next?"

"We got Ree Helper on our side. That's our big point. She can pull Weakspoon around where she wants him because she plays up to him. She's been playing hide-and-go-seek with Bates and Jones to lure them out of town. We got to make that pair believe we're their friends."

John Walker's smile was not pretty. "We ain't makin' much progress that way, Bart, it seems to me. Bates nailed you with his jug and knocked you cold, remember?"

"Can I forget it? Well, she'll pull Bates and Jones out of town, and that will be the end of them — if we can stage the right ambush. Bury them in the badlands and the law will never find them out in the rough country."

"That the deal, then?"

"At the present time, yes."

Walker blew smoke and regarded it with ironic amusement, his smile small and tight against his thin lips.

"You're forgettin' one man, Bart."

"I am? Who?"

"This heavy-set gent, this stranger, this gink who calls himself Mike Jacobs. That fella ain't hangin' around here for his health. He might be an advance man for the railroad, tryin' to sneak Thunder

Canyon away from Ree Helper. Good luck we got the tip about the railroad in time — "

"Ree Helper is the smart one on that point, not us. She had the good luck to work in the railroad's Chicago office and she got the inside dope on Thunder Canyon. But what about this gent Mike Jacobs?"

"We got to get rid of him," John Walker said. "What does Ree say about him? She must have some opinion about him, hasn't she?"

"She figures he's an advance man. She never saw him around the office, she told me, but we know danged well he's out here to buy land in Thunder Canyon. He hasn't approached her yet, but she is working toward that point, she tells me. He'll find land hard to buy in Thunder."

John Walker watched, saying nothing.

Bart Terry's boots made sounds against the floor.

"We've got a million bucks in our hands, John. When the railroad gets through Thunder Canyon, then they can develop the copper mines — but we'll own those mines and the railroad will have to dicker with us on our terms. Mind that big mesa in the bottom of Thunder Canyon? Right where the Helper house is located?"

"Yes."

"Well, that'll be where we build the town. I can see it now — streets and houses — and we'll own all the gambling and the women. We'll own the town, in fact. Terryville, we'll call it."

"You still got to get around Ree Helper. She owns the homestead and desert claim and mining claim rights to all that territory. It ain't yours yet; it belongs to Ree."

Bart Terry smiled slowly. "I'll marry her and get that land . . . or kill her and forge deeds," he said quietly. "The minute she turns against me I kill her, even if she is a woman."

John Walker looked at his knuckles. "She'll come around, Bart. She's got brains. She showed that when she hurried to this country and took up them claims so she could control Thunder Canyon."

Terry continued pacing.

"We got to get rid of Bates. Get that rifle and the silencer and go out and kill him — Wait a minute, John!"

They stood there, tense and taut, with Bart Terry holding onto John Walker's forearm, both killers poised and listening to the sounds out in the alley. For a woman had screamed, "There's a man out here — dead — "

Other sounds were heard — running boots, the babble of voices. Bart Terry looked at John Walker, and his smile was a twisted, ugly thing.

"They've found Bates out there, John. Well, we can't kill him now . . . Who was thet dame that hollered like that?"

"Right off, I'd say the voice belonged to Imogene Carter. Sounded like her, Bart."

They listened again. John Walker started toward the back door, but Bart Terry reached out and grabbed him and stopped him.

"What's the matter, Bart?"

"Don't go out that door. Go out the front."

John Walker nodded. They went into the brightly lighted interior of the saloon, and a young girl, pretty despite her garish paint, came up to Terry, taking him by the arm and smiling up at him.

"Something is going on out in the alley, honey."

A man stuck his head in the front door. "They found the new Judge out in the alley, Bart. Done drunk hisself unconscious. Stinks from likker like a distiller's vat."

Terry essayed surprise. "John and I were playing checkers in the side room. We heard the noise but thought it was a ruckus here in the saloon." He looked at his gunman. "We'd best get around to the back, eh, John?"

"Never did see a drunk judge," Walker said, grinning.

There was quite a crowd around the judge when the two arrived. With Bart Terry in the lead, they pushed through the crowd, Terry pushing people rudely to one side. Judge Bates was just coming to. Walker had sure sprinkled the jurist with whisky. Imogene Carter was kneeling beside the judge. Somebody had brought a pail of cold well water, and Imogene was washing the judge's forehead with her wet handkerchief.

"Where is the doc?" Terry asked.

Imogene said, "He's out on a drunk somewhere, they tell me."

Terry said, "Two drunks in town now — the doctor and the judge. John, get on that side of him, and I'll take this side, and we'll tote the souse into the Bucket of Suds."

They got the weak-kneed jurist between them, and Bart Terry, always the gambler, knew that their gamble had been successful. The mumblings of the gathered townspeople told him that. It was a disgrace that the district attorney send them an old drunk to solve a case as important as the Helper case! What an example to parade before the young people of Muletown!

With Judge Bates stumbling between them, Bart Terry and John Walker got him out on the main street, with Imogene Carter watching and following. And from across the street, hidden by the night, another woman watched — the woman known as Ree Helper. And Ree Helper held a .45 in her small and feminine hand . . .

8

JUDGE BATES remembered lurching along, held up by two men, one on each side, and he remembered hearing a woman's voice. He wanted to get to his room and talk with Tobacco. But yonder came his partner now, pushing through the crowd with reckless haste, elbowing this man and that, his face worried and tired-looking.

"Heard about your misfortune, Bates. Come on up to the room an' rest. Just got word about your trouble or I'da bin here sooner."

"Who told you, Tobacco?"

"That gal, Ree Helper, told me."

Judge Bates stumbled. Surprise had almost knocked his knees out from under his thick body.

"She come to the hotel room, Tobacco?"

"She sure did, Bates. Walk careful, man, 'cause this ground is bumpy,

99

and your laigs — ”

"Forget my legs! Tell me about Ree!"

"She come to the hotel room an' knocked. Told me about them findin' you cold in thet alley! Who slugged you, Bates?"

They were just entering the hotel lobby. The lamplight washed across Tobacco Jones' rugged face, giving it a sad and tragic appearance.

"Who slugged you, Bates?"

That question had also been bothering the jurist.

The first person who came into his mind as a suspect was, of course, none other than the sterling rancher and saloon-keeper, one Bart Terry. This was only logical. His jug, swung at the right moment and with the right force, had tumbled Bart Terry off his boots and into the sawdust of the Bucket of Suds Saloon. By all rights, Terry had a reason for slugging him.

"It wasn't Bart Terry, I am sure of that. Deadly sure, Tobacco."

Tobacco Jones chewed and squinted.

"What makes you make that cocksure statement, Bates? How come you're so sure it weren't this skunk of a Bart Terry?"

"I had seen Terry just a moment before, and Terry had had his hands full. Arms full, in fact."

"Doin' what, Bates?"

"Kissing your girl friend, namely Ree Helper."

Tobacco Jones studied him coldly. "Did that rap on your noggin addle you completely, Bates? Or is your eyes seein' things what ain't there?"

The judge told about seeing the pair in the alley.

"Then I go on a few rods and bingo — this gent comes behind me and slugs me cold. I got a glimpse of him but couldn't recognize him."

"Somebody coming down the hall."

The visitor proved to be the heavy-set man named Mike Jacobs. He and some townsmen, he related, had got lanterns and had looked over the place in the alley where His Honor had fallen, and they had seen nothing pointing to the identity of his assailant. The alley was dusty; bootprints were all over.

Judge Bates said, "Thank you, sir, for your courtesy and consideration."

"Just thought you'd like to know, Your Honor."

"Again, thanks."

For some reason Mike Jacobs seemed loath to leave. He looked from one man to the other, and when the silence got too heavy he said, "Good night, gentlemen." Then he was moving ponderously down the hall.

"Odd duck," Tobacco Jones said. "I made some inquiries of old Bald Head, the clerk downstairs. This Jacobs gent just came here out of nowhere a while back, hangs around an' drinks not a drop, plays cards a little, and never says much. Now why did he come up here to our room?"

"To tell me he had looked for tracks."

"Hogwash, Bates, hogwash. He's tied up in this some way, an' I'll bet we run into him again later on."

"Maybe you're right."

The judge sat on the bed. Next door somebody dropped a shoe. Then another shoe, and a door closed somewhere. The hotel walls were paper thin and sound traveled unhampered through them.

"Somebody else comin'," Tobacco said.

This time their visitor proved to be more attractive to the eye than had the bulky personage of one Mike Jacobs.

"Why, Miss Lou," the judge told the little waitress. "You're a sight for sore eyes, as the old saying goes."

The waitress smiled, eyes crinkling.

"I brought you some headache powders, Judge."

Judge Bates looked at Tobacco and winked. "Sure nice of you, honey. My head feels like a herd of buffalo are beating across my brain."

She went to the table and poured water out of the big pitcher into the glass. She had a nice back — a very attractive back. She turned, holding the glass, the water now white with powder. "Drink this quick, Judge Bates."

103

"Maybe you're trying to poison me," he joked.

"I wouldn't poison you. I'd like to get hold of a man like you. I already know your salary — got the figures from the courthouse. I know you're single too." She was smiling good-naturedly but under that smile was a sincerity that her smile could not belie.

"You sure must want to get out of that café," Tobacco Jones said.

"I wanta keep house for a good man," she said.

Out in the hall, feet shuffled, and somebody knocked on a door down the hall, and the squeaky voice of the clerk said, "Here's the hot water for your bath."

They heard a door open and close. Then the clerk shuffled off, going down the protesting stairs.

"Somebody," said Tobacco Jones, "is spoilin' the night by takin' a bath, and at this ungodly hour — all of nine o'clock."

The judge had drunk the water. Already

he felt better. He smiled and thanked Lou, who seemed very happy. He thanked her again, she smiled again, and then she said, "Gosh, nine o'clock already. I'd best stampede out. In a hotel room with two strange men — what would my dead mother think if she were alive? Goo'-bye."

She scooted out, slipped down the hall, and was gone.

"Another woman on your string," Tobacco grunted. "Me, I'm jealous, Bates." He cocked his head. "Gawd, another visitor."

This time the knock was masculine — strong and loud. Tobacco opened the door and John Walker stuck in his head with, "How goes it, Bates? Terry sent me over to see if you want anything — "

Walker's words stopped suddenly. Tobacco Jones had clipped him on the jaw. He knocked him out in the hall and Walker sat down. Tobacco got his guns and gave them to Judge Bates, who had followed them into the hall.

Finally Walker blurted, "What in the

name of blazes is wrong with you, Jones? Why did you slug me, you fool?"

Judge Bates saw Tobacco Jones' long face take on a deliberate look of amazement. He had trouble stifling his own grin, and with difficulty His Honor kept his wide face bland.

"Yes, Jones, what's the matter with you?" the judge chimed in. "Here this man merely comes as a neighbor to inquire about me — and you haul off and knock him on his seat!"

"Did I hit him, Bates?"

Judge Bates saw a strained look come across the face of gunman John Walker. Plainly the gundog was wondering about the sanity of one postmaster named Tobacco Jones. Slowly Walker got to his feet. He wiped his mouth with the back of his sleeve and looked at his guns, still in Judge Bates' possession.

"If you don't mind, Your Honor, I'll take my guns, please?"

"Oh, sure." Judge Bates handed Walker the two Colts, muzzles pointing at the man, who moved to one side so that if a gun did discharge, the bullet would miss him. "I'm sorry, Walker, but my partner is not — well, his mentality is not too stable — "

Tobacco still showed that surprised look. He was, the judge realized, an excellent actor.

"I don't remember hitting this man, Bates. My mind — it must be going — Look, a woman!"

The door to the next room had opened. The head and shoulders of a woman looked out. The woman proved to be Imogene Carter.

"Really, gentlemen, I'd like to finish my bath, please, without getting a bullet through the wall. Would you do that for me?"

John Walker bowed. "You can expect no trouble from me, madam."

"Nor us, either," Judge Bates assured her.

Her smile was sweetness itself. "Oh, thank you, Judge."

Then the door was shut.

John Walker said, "I almost forgot

my achin' jaw." He glared at Tobacco, who looked back at him with dull eyes. "There's no use my makin' a threat against this gent, not until his mind comes back."

"If it ever comes back," His Honor said solemnly.

Tobacco said, "Oh, my head — it's spinnin'!" and he darted into the room, throwing himself on the bed. John Walker, rubbing his jaw, hastily departed, shaking his head. Judge Bates went back into the room. Tobacco Jones lay on the bed, shaking with laughter. The judge, remembering the dazed, stunned, fearful look in Walker's eyes, laughed, too. He sat down and laughed and then, without warning, he said suddenly, "What's that noise, Jones?"

"Noise? Me, laughin'!"

"No, in that clothes closet."

Tobacco Jones sat up, slender body poised, head cocked. "Sounds like somebody movin' in that closet. I'll look — "

He got to his feet, glancing first at

their shotguns that leaned against the far wall. He intended to tiptoe toward the closet, jerk open the door. But his plan did not materialize.

Somebody inside the clothes closet came into wild and active life. A door slammed inside the narrow confines, and this brought both partners forward. Tobacco ripped open the door and then, for the first time, the partners were aware of a door inside the closet, leading to the next room. Evidently these two rooms at one time had been part of a duplex; a closet had been built between them, changing them into single rooms.

The door was vibrating. Judge Bates, shotgun in hand, barged into the room, Tobacco on his heels. He was in a room gaudy with feminine doodads, and he realized he was in Imogene Carter's room.

From a side room, came the whoops of a woman, and he thought, Imogene Carter, taking a bath. But his interest was on the door that led into the hall. That door was just closing. He caught a brief glimpse of a pair of faded levis, and then the door was slammed shut without allowing him further view of the person who had hidden in the clothes closet.

"Halt, you, halt!"

Suddenly Imogene Carter looked out fearfully from the side room. "Oh, you two again! What the heck are you doing in my room — "

"Somebody in the clothes closet ran through here — in the hall now — "

"You're crazy!"

By now, Tobacco Jones and Judge Bates, shotguns bristling, were in the hall. Again, the judge glimpsed the marauder, a flash of blue levis — this time, the person was ducking in another door down the hall. And His Honor stopped, bringing up his shotgun. His plan was to fire into the door and scare the person into stopping or surrendering.

His hammer fell. The firing-pin snapped against the shotgun cartridge. But there was no roar. Just the click of the firing-pin hitting the cartridge in the shotgun's barrel.

Tobacco Jones, also, had let his hammer fall. And the only thing he received in reply was also the click of the firing-pin snapping against the shotgun cartridge's metal case.

"Our shotguns — somethin' wrong — "

Judge Bates jerked open the door. The room was empty and dark. Across the room was an open window. The breeze pushed back the curtain slightly, and a street light showed the outline of the window. The bottom pane was open. The marauder had slipped out the window onto the roof of the building next door.

The judge rapped out his instructions. "Somebody has doctored our guns. Then we came back to our room too soon — trapped them in the clothes closet — Whoever it was, they went out that window."

"I'll go down the back — meet you in the alley."

"Watch out, Tobacco. That shotgun is no good, an' don't forget it — "

"Dirty scum!"

The postmaster wheeled and ran back down the hallway, heading for the rear stairs that led from the second story of the hotel to the alley. Judge Bates hustled his bulk through the window and dropped to the roof of the building. The building was old, the roof sagged under his weight, and for a moment he was afraid of going through the roof. But although the roof sagged terrible, it held him. He hurried across it, heading for the next building. But no building abutted this one: there was a sheer drop of about twelve feet into a vacant lot. Panting, the judge looked around, but he saw no sign of the marauder.

Below him, a man walked by on the street, and he saw that it was Sheriff Olaf Engstrand, apparently making a round of the town before turning in. The sheriff did not hear him, so he did not look up as he passed out of sight, moving down the street in his slow and lumbering manner.

The judge dropped to the ground, bending his knees to break his fall.

Shotgun under arm, he hurried back toward the alley, where he found his partner talking to a man. At first, because of the darkness, His Honor could not recognize the man but as he got closer, he saw it was Bart Terry.

"Howdy, Your Honor. Shotgun and all, eh? Out huntin' midnight jackrabbits?" Terry was very congenial.

"Yes, Terry. Hunting jackrabbits."

Tobacco explained, "Met this gent back here in the alley, Judge Bates. He claims he was comin' over to the hotel to apologize for John Walker swingin' on me just because I accidentally said somethin' he didn't cotton to."

The jurist nodded soberly. "Walker took a poke at Tobacco because Jones said something that meant nothing at all. Jones knocked him down. Thanks for coming over to apologize, Terry. We accept in good faith. But surely you aren't responsible for another grown man's flippancy, are you?"

Terry spoke stiffly. "Walker works for me. This sure seems odd, Your

Honor — you two a-totin' your scatterguns out a-huntin' rabbits at this time of the night. You mean that — for sure?"

His voice held the same bewilderment that had rimmed John Walker's. Darkness hid His Honor's smile.

"That's right, and goodnight for now, Terry."

"Good — Goodnight."

They left Terry standing there. They were silent as they climbed the back stairway. They said nothing as they went down the hall. When they got inside the room, Tobacco said, "He figures our brains has slipped their picket pins, Bates. Lord, did you hear his voice — thought sure he was talkin' to a coupla nuts, he did! We got him on the run!"

"Maybe."

Tobacco sobered, his face glum. "Yeah, he's tough, he is." He sat down and shoved out his long legs and looked at his boots. "You catch any sight of thet fella what hid in the clothes closet?"

"No, nothing more."

"It weren't Terry, 'cause he didn't wear levis. Whoever it was was up here to doctor our guns. Lord, we could have got kilt, Bates!"

They broke their sawed-off shotguns. Twin cartridges flipped out and were caught for minute study. Firing pins had landed correctly and with proper force, denting the brass ring. By all tokens the cartridges should not have failed to fire.

The ends had been opened, and the beebees and powder poured out, rendering them harmless. And when Judge Bates looked at Tobacco Jones the postmaster read the bitter anger in his partner's eyes.

"Had we gone against a set of guns, Tobacco, we would have been shot down like defenseless coyotes! Somebody aimed to job us to death, friend. While you were out to see me, this devil did his work. We came back early, and he slipped into that closet, and finally had to make a break for it — and he got away."

"Another visitor coming."

This time the visitor proved to be a pretty one. Imogene Carter wore a dressing robe that accentuated her loveliness. She was barefooted and she smelled of a nice perfume. She had come over to apologize. She had not meant to holler at them as she had, using such a high-pitched tone of voice. Tobacco quickly noticed she talked to Judge Bates, occasionally sending him a glance.

"Your apologies, Imogene, are accepted."

"I don't understand — "

"Neither do we," His Honor informed her. "Now for a night of good sleep, far from the cares of the day, Imogene."

She took the hint and said goodnight. When the door had closed Tobacco grunted, "Imogene now, eh? Bates, one of these women — they'll get the best of you yet — I'm mad, Bates."

"Only dogs get mad, chum."

Tobacco dropped his boot loudly. "I hate to bunk down with you, Bates. You snore and you ride broncs all night. We should've got a room with two beds. Is that somebody else a-comin' this way?"

Boots again sounded in the hall.

Another visitor. But this one was a sad-looking Nordic, tired from the saddle. Sheriff Olaf Engstrand did not sit down. He balanced himself on his long legs, raking each with a glance, and finally the glance settled on Judge Bates.

"I was out to that holdup spot. Never found a thing. Tried to locate Doc Goodenough, curse his black soul, to see if he treated anybody for buckshot wounds — but where the devil is he?"

"Nobody seems to know," the judge said.

Engstrand said, "They tell me you got clipped cold back in the alley, judge? Or was it really drink that knocked you out?" Olaf Engstrand had weak and watery eyes.

The judge was on his feet, fists doubled. Engstrand stepped back, fear in those watery eyes.

"You aim to hit me, Bates? I'm the sheriff — "

"Get out and let me sleep!"

"You can't boss the sheriff — "

The judge's pudgy right hand shot out. Fingers fastened tightly around Engstrand's star. One jerk, quick and concise; cloth tore, and the badge was in His Honor's grip.

"You aren't sheriff any longer, Engstrand."

Engstrand's eyes became hard for a moment, and Tobacco Jones, watching the man, thought he would hit. But plainly he was a stooge for Bart Terry, and without Terry present to back him, his spine was water.

"You're only jokin', Judge?"

Judge Bates nodded. "Sure, just joking. Now get out and let us sleep."

"I lost my patience, I guess. I'll take my badge back."

"You'll get it when I'm good and ready to give it back to you. You forgot that I am the county judge and I'm your boss. Goodnight, Engstrand."

"My badge — "

"Get out!"

"See you in the morning," Engstrand said, and left.

Tobacco Jones shut the door and bolted it. He said slowly, "I dunno, Bates, whether that was right or wrong. This county ain't got no sheriff now since you peeled the badge off Engstrand."

"You're wrong there, Tobacco."

Tobacco watched his partner suspiciously. He did not like the glow in His Honor's eyes.

"Bates, you tore the star off that gink, and he ain't sheriff — so who is the sheriff of this county?"

"You are."

Tobacco Jones chewed with slow regularity, eyes slitted in speculation. He was gaunt, silent, and tough as he watched his partner.

"I'm sheriff?"

"I just appointed you sheriff. The county judge can appoint a sheriff if the sheriff dies, is killed, or quits in his term."

"I'm the law."

Judge Bates rolled off his sock and got into bed.

"Close your mouth, and let me sleep!"

9

JUDGE BATES became aware of somebody banging on the door. His Honor sat up and said, "Who is there?"

"Engstrand."

Judge Bates, wide awake, smiled. Engstrand had almost used the word *Sheriff,* but had caught himself in time. Tobacco Jones stirred, sat up, blinked and asked, "What is it, Bates?"

"Engstrand at the door."

"Let the fool in, Bates, afore he pounds the door off'n its hinges! You can hear him all the way to Cheyenne the way he's hollerin'!"

Judge Bates pulled on his pants and waddled to the door. Engstrand had eyes as wild as those of a boogered bronc who had just had a saddle cinched onto his back for the first time.

"They shot him — They done shot Weakspoon!"

120

The judge regarded the ex-sheriff with a hard glance. "Look, man, quit your joking, please. Weakspoon is in a jail cell. We own the keys to the jail. We took them off you last night, remember?"

"My deputy had a set. I got them from him this morning. I went to clean out my desk — I heard him moanin'. Somebody shot him while he lay asleep. I told you you shouldn't have locked him up."

"How bad is he hurt?" Tobacco Jones demanded, dressing hurriedly.

"I dunno. Doc Goodenough — he ain't in town. Just when we needs him — "

Judge Bates was pulling on his shirt. "How would anybody get into the jail?" he demanded. "We have one set of keys and you have another. Are there any more keys floating around?"

"I dunno."

The judge buttoned his shirt, flipped it under his belt, and looked at Tobacco, who was pulling on his boots. "Now why, Tobacco, would anybody want to shoot Weakspoon?"

"To kill him, of course."

"But why kill him?"

Tobacco Jones stood up, jerking on his shirt. "He's tied up in this mess of hell some way, Bates. You know what?"

"What?"

"I figure that Bart Terry's gunman was actin' for Terry an' Walker, an' they had sicked him onto Weakspoon, hopin' to kill the lawyer, but the shyster turned the tables."

"That's nothing new. That's why I jugged Weakspoon. To protect him by bars. I aimed to question him today, too. Well, he can still talk."

"If he wants to," Tobacco Jones finished sagely.

"You men talk sorta crazy," Engstrand said. "I still think you cain't take my star away from me, Bates."

Judge Bates said, "Look on Tobacco's shirt, fella. What is that thing you see pinned there?"

Engstrand looked, his eyes mean and small. "My star," he admitted. He said to the world at large, "A judge can do anything he wants, eh? Even be illegal in some of his dealings, that it, Bates?"

"He can make his deals legal, you mean."

While dressing, the judge, although carrying on a running conversation, had not been idle mentally. Somebody had shot Weakspoon after opening a door to the jail. Or had he been shot by a gun poked through the window?

He put this question to Engstrand.

"I looked for marks outside his winder, Bates. The winder is up high an' a man would have to stand on a ladder to look in, an' I found no marks of no ladder. The winder is so high a man on hossback couldn't look in even if he stretched hisself on his stirrups."

"The killer — or would-be killer — had to come in a door, eh?"

"Sure did. Back door, I figure."

"Why figure that?"

"Oh, just a hunch. Weakspoon don't remember nothin'. Remembers bein' shot, but he claims he saw nobody — somebody shot from the hallway, he says. That also eliminates the winder angle."

The judge asked, "About what time did it happen?"

"Weakspoon don't know. He was knocked out for a spell, I guess. Bullet hit him in the chest, low down — right above his guts. He bled like a sticked hog. Blood all over everything."

"I'm ready to travel," Tobacco said.

They got their shotguns. They banged down the hallway, boots pounding; they brought Imogene Carter to the door. When they rounded the corner to go downstairs to the lobby, His Honor looked back and saw Imogene's pretty head sticking out of the door.

The judge's watch said a few minutes after five. Dawn was brilliant, kissing the earth, which had cooled during the night. There was no breeze, but the air was cool, being refrigerated by the snow-tipped peaks. But when noon came, the earth, His Honor knew, would be blistering hot.

Judge Bates frowned, troubled by the enormity of this problem. Tobacco Jones chewed thoughtfully, his long face almost savage-looking in the dawn. Engstrand walked down the alley with such a hard stride it was as if he bore a grudge against the soil and wanted to drive his bootheels deep into it.

"My ol' lady — she guv me a rough time, men. Kept me awake all night jawin' at me — an' she can use her jaw, too. She aims to talk to you two."

"What about?" Tobacco Jones asked, knowing full well what the answer would be.

"She wants you two to give me my star back. She claims her an' the kids will starve to death, an' she might be right. Until I got this county job I wasn't much of a provider. I get my star back and I'll work like blazes on this case, men."

"You sure of that?" Judge Bates asked.

"I'll work my tail down to a nubbin, Your Honor."

They came to the back door of the jail. Engstrand had relocked the door. Tobacco Jones, using his key, opened it. Engstrand said slowly, "There might be only two keys to this door. I got one, you got the other."

"Don't start that talk," Judge Bates warned sternly. "We never had no call to shoot Weakspoon. We put him in jail to protect him, not get him penned up for a shooting. You start that talk around town, and I'll twist you around until you can lick the bottom of your feet with your tongue!"

Engstrand turned purple. "I never meant it the way you took it, Your Honor."

"I mean just what I said," Judge Bates said angrily.

Engstrand led the way inside. The cells were fairly well illuminated, for the dawn was seeping through, but with such small high windows, very little daylight ever, at any time, penetrated the cell block. Engstrand stamped down the concrete, big boots shuffling, and behind him traveled Judge Bates, shotgun akimbo. And trailing His Honor came tobacco-chewing Tobacco Jones, his long face creased by serious lines.

"Here is his cell, gents."

Lawyer Weakspoon had really lost blood. The sheet was covered, his skin was covered, and he was very pale. He looked up, and his glance became flint hard.

"You devils put me in here, and somebody shot me!"

"We didn't mean it that way." Judge Bates was on his knees, studying the wound. The bullet had torn through the man's flank. Evidently he had been lying on his side and the lead, whistling in, had hit him high and below the ribs, ripping through flesh and possibly puncturing entrails. The man must have spent a terrible night, alone and needing help.

"I called for help, after I come to," the lawyer said, "but nobody heard me. Then I lost more blood and I passed out."

"Who shot you?" His Honor asked, eyes on the lawyer's blood-drained face.

"I don't know."

"Tell us what happened?" Engstrand asked.

Judge Bates said, "That can wait until

after we get him out of here. No use trying to question him here in the condition he is in."

Engstrand's deputy came down the corridor. He had just eaten a big breakfast and looked cheerful. But at the sight of Lawyer Weakspoon, his cheerfulness fled.

"Where were you last night, Deputy?" Judge Bates asked.

The man had been home in bed. He had his wife to attest to that fact, he said. He and Weakspoon were good friends, and Engstrand corroborated this statement. The deputy and Weakspoon were checker addicts.

"He never shot me," Weakspoon said sourly. "Either one of you two hellions sneaked in to salt me down, or else somebody else has a key to the clink."

"We hold nothing against you," Judge Bates said. "Common logic will tell a man of your intelligence that, Weakspoon."

"Get me out of here," the lawyer said.

Judge Bates sent Engstrand and the deputy to Doc Goodenough's office to look for a stretcher. His Honor then scouted around, looking for signs pointing toward the identity of the ambusher, but he found none. The floor, made of cement, showed nothing; if he had identified his killer, Weakspoon kept it to himself. For some reason His Honor got the impression that maybe Weakspoon had identified his assailant, but was keeping this information to himself. He must have had some idea as to the identity of the rifleman, but this information he kept locked tightly behind his thin lips.

"Here they come with a stretcher," Tobacco Jones said.

With the ex-lawman and the deputy came two other men, nobody other than Bart Terry and John Walker, who asked questions and learned nothing more than did Judge Bates and Tobacco Jones.

"You two are out of sougans early," His Honor pointed out.

"Spent the night out to the ranch, too," Bart Terry answered. "Even rid in from there this morning. We're early birds, eh, John?"

"We're hard to beat," Walker said pointedly.

The judge held the lawyer by the shoulders, Tobacco Jones got him by both feet, and Bart Terry and John Walker held him from sagging in the middle, while Engstrand and the deputy held the rails of the stretcher. When the lawyer was finally in place, they marched down the street, turned into the hotel, and the clerk showed them to a downstairs room, evidently used as a hospital room. It was big and cheery and had a hard bed.

"Wish we knew for sure where Doc Goodenough is," Engstrand said anxiously. "This man is bad hurt. Do you figure he is out to the Widder's, Deputy?"

"I can ride out there and see for sure."

Bart Terry was washing his hands at the washstand, for he had got some of Weakspoon's blood on him.

"The Widder has her boy out on the hill all the time, an' the kid watches with field glasses when Doc is there. Anybody ride that way, and the kid gives the alarm, and she hides Doc out in the brush or somewhere."

"I'll go see," the deputy said.

Judge Bates washed the wound with warm water, then used some antiseptic found in the medico's office. The bullet had gone straight through. Infection, His Honor figured, would be the big enemy. Engstrand got a matronly woman, evidently a midwife to attend the lawyer. She also knew something about bandaging and, with the aid of Judge Bates, the lawyer was resting as comfortably as possible, a neat bandage around his middle.

Judge Bates and Tobacco went toward Lou's restaurant. Imogene Carter, radiant, was already at the counter, and her pretty hand went out to rest on the stool next to her, signifying she was holding it for Lemanuel Bates. The judge thanked her and slid onto the stool, showing Lou a big smile, something he had not given to Imogene. And Imogene, noticing this, allowed the trace of a scowl to move across her forehead. Lou saw this, too, and, unnoticed by Imogene, she winked at His Honor, who winked back.

"What will it be for breakfast, honey?" Lou asked the judge.

Honey . . . Imogene was suddenly and completely immersed in her hotcakes. Tobacco, who had seen the wink, grinned widely, keeping his face away from Imogene, who seemed to hate her hotcakes, for she dug into them savagely with the side of her fork, a very unladylike gesture.

"I'll take bloaters," Tobacco Jones said ungraciously. "Make them as thick as saddle-blankets, Lou, but not as tough. Then give me lots of sirup for 'em, eh?"

Lou nodded, eyes still on His Honor. "And for you, sweetheart?"

Imogene finally looked up. "My, you two sure use loving words."

"We're in love," Judge Bates intoned.

"We've known each other all of twenty hours, isn't it, Lou?"

"No, about sixteen, I figure."

Lou was almost laughing. His Honor also had a tough time keeping a straight face as he followed Tobacco's lead and ordered hotcakes and trimmings.

They tied into their chuck. Imogene kept switching the conversation around to the shooting of Jack Weakspoon. After a while, she got tired of getting no answers, so she paid and left. Judge Bates glanced at her straight, pretty back.

"You're kind of rough on her," Lou said. "After all, Your Honor, she is your secretary."

"My what?"

Lou looked at him in surprise. "Didn't you know she was the court stenographer, sir, and also your secretary?"

"I sure didn't."

Tobacco Jones got his mouth around about half a hotcake, and his words came out mumbled and uncertain.

"More doggone trouble, Bates."

They finished eating and joked for a

while, but trade was coming in, so Lou hadn't much time. The partners paid and went outside. Just at that moment two riders came down the street, broncs at a lope. They pulled in fast, dust rising, and one hollered, "Hey, that's the judge who sentenced us to Rawlin's pen, fella! That's the dirty skunk, for sure!"

"Sure is! Judge Bates!"

And then, without further warning, it happened.

10

A HORSE rearing, pawing against the cruelty of a spade bit, and his scream was loud in protest. Dust swiveled in, strong and gray, and the rider of the rearing horse had his .45 out of leather, sunlight moving angrily across the rising barrel.

Judge Bates hollered, "Move out, Tobacco, and shoot to kill!"

One rider — the one astraddle the pinto — screamed, "I'll kill Jones, Spud! Jones's my triggermeat — !"

A woman screamed. Lou, in the café, watched through the window, pulled toward the window by the roaring threat of a gunman's savage voice. The sound registered on Judge Lemanuel Bates, shrill and filled with warning, and from the corner of his right eye, he saw Tobacco Jones sprawl out, flat on his belly, on the plank sidewalk, shotgun slamming upward against his shoulder.

Then His Honor was in action. On one knee, his shotgun rising. Across the neck of the rearing sorrel came the ugly stab of gunfire from a .45 Colt. The gunman was low, and the sudden rearing of his sorrel threw his lead wide, or else Judge Bates might have died, blood seeping the soil of that dusty mountain street. As it was, the bullet was low, plowing into the board sidewalk.

The judge fired. The shotgun roared, stock kicking back against the jurist's wide shoulder. And a shotgun, at such close range, was a terrible weapon — capable of putting a hole the size of a man's fist through a man. And the beebees, bunched because of the close range, tore a hole that big in the gunman's chest.

It knocked him from his bronc. The horse went backwards, rolled on him, and its four legs kicked wildly. Judge Bates, shotgun smoking, swung the weapon on the other gunman, but already he was fleeing. Bent low over his horse, he roared down the street, heading for the safety created by distance. And Tobacco Jones, shotgun to shoulder, was ready to shoot again.

"Don't," His Honor hollered. "You'll hit an innocent horse at that range."

The rider, spurring as if the devil were chasing him with a hot pitchfork, slanted his cayuse around the far corner and was gone, with only dust rising to show he had ever been on the street.

Tobacco lowered the shotgun, and his sunken eyes were savage. "I got him hard but he never got knocked out of kak. He was slow, and I shot him afore he could shoot, I reckon."

"He got in a shot."

"Never knew that, Bates."

"After you shot him, his pistol went off."

"Never got close to me. Let's look at this bucko you winged. Look at his sorrel run!"

The horse was pounding away, stirrups flapping, bridle reins trailing. He was wise, and he ran with his head wide to one side so he would not trip himself on his dragging bridle reins.

The town, silent the moment before, was now pounding with action, with the rise and lift of voices. Dogs had come awake, and now they barked with a roaring cacophony of uplifted noses. The deputy came running, and Judge Bates ordered, "Follow that man who got away, Deputy!"

"I'll do that, Your Honor!"

The deputy untied a horse from a hitchrack and hit the stirrups and loped away, riding like a jockey with his knees high, for he had taken a horse with a saddle that had very short stirrups. He whipped the bony bronc for speed, and the corner soon hid him, just as it had hid the fleeing gunman.

They went forward, reloading their shotguns, and then they stood over the gunman who had tried to kill His Honor. The man lay limp in the bloody dust, mangled by the bronc and the saddle as the horse had reared over backwards. The judge went to both knees, rolling the man over. A long face, thick with whiskers, looked up at him, but the eyes did no looking — they were dull and coated with dust and death was in them.

"Dead," His Honor said, getting to his feet.

Tobacco Jones' voice was not too steady. "The one gent hollered thet you had sent him an' his pard to the pen in Rawlins, Bates. You recognize this dead gent, eh?"

"I sure don't. He's a stranger to me. I saw him yesterday when we first came to Muletown."

"You saw him? Where at?"

"Down at the depot platform when we unloaded that poor drummer. This gent stood right close to me and made no move to git at me then."

"You figure you sentenced him to the pen?"

"I never had him in court. I know all the faces I've had in my court. I've only been a judge for a few years now and I got a memory for faces, as well you know."

"You never forgit them."

Lou said, "Come on inside, men, and have some coffee."

"Later," His Honor said.

A group of riders swept down the street, heading out to follow the deputy and the man whom Tobacco Jones had wounded. Other people stood around the dead man. Somebody had caught the dead man's fleeing bronc and had led him back. Judge Bates saw that the horse bore a Rocking H brand.

"Is there a Rocking H Ranch around here?" he asked a man.

"No brand like that around here. Must be a Texas horse, I'd say — there's a Rockin' H brand down out of Lubbock."

"You know this dead man, sir?"

"Never seen him afore in my life."

Somebody said the man had been hanging around town for about a week. He had left yesterday evening, this informant said, and everybody thought he and his partner were pulling stakes. The judge glanced at Bart Terry and John Walker, who stood and listened.

"Either of you fellows know this dead man?"

Bart Terry's eyes were deadpan. "He hung around my saloon for a few days. I talked to him once but got nothing out of him. Close-mouthed, he was; so was his partner. Drifters, I took them for, and let it go at that."

Judge Bates looked at John Walker.

"Played poker with him one day," Walker said. "Asked no questions, got no answers — and he won around a hundred bucks off me, the lucky dog."

"He'll win no more Pots," Judge Bates growled. "He's raking in the devil's Pot now somewhere over the Ridge." His Honor stabbed a sudden glance at Bart Terry. "What do you know about this dead gents pard?"

"Not a thing. Never even talked to him."

"And you, Walker?"

Walker snarled, "What is this — an inquest?" He did not await an answer. "I talked with him once — rather, I tried to talk with him. All he did was grunt

141

like a Berkshire boar."

Lou said, "Don't forget that coffee, Judge Bates."

The judge nodded. Tobacco said to Engstrand, "Get the carcass off the street, Olaf."

"I'm not the law," Engstrand said surlily.

Tobacco said, "You're my deputy. As of this moment, you're my deputy. You and the deputy tote the stiff off the street, and do it pronto. Might poison some of the local houseflies!"

"We gotta think of the houseflies," His Honor said. Engstrand hollered for his deputy, who had just returned. The deputy dismounted, all importance, and he let a little suspense build up before he said, "Well, I got him. They're bringin' in his carcass."

"We heard no shots," His Honor reminded him.

Bart Terry asked, "Has he said anything?"

The deputy said, "He hasn't, an' he won't, Bart. You see, he fell dead off'n

142

his bronc. He started to sag, an' then lie toppled, an' I come up, gun out — but he was pitch dead, he was."

Terry hesitated, looked at John Walker and said, "Too bad, Bates. You boys are liquid hell with them shotguns, I can see that."

"We've had a little practice." The judge spoke modestly.

"We gotta git this stiff off'n the street," Engstrand told the deputy. "I'm a deputy now, Jones tells me."

They toted the dead man off the dust, with the limp body sagging in the middle. Judge Bates, now his normal self, went into the café, with Tobacco trailing. The rest of the town awaited the arrival of the other dead man. Some went out to meet the riders bringing in the carcass.

Lou poured coffee. His Honor noticed that her hands trembled.

"First time a stranger has ever tried to kill me," Judge Bates said. "What do you know about this dead gent, girl?"

"Just what you already know. They ate

143

in here twice, that's all — tough-looking men, with whiskers — ugh!"

"Somethin's burnin' in the kitchen," Tobacco said.

"My roast!"

Lou fled toward the kitchen, grabbing a dish towel on the way. The swinging doors swished behind her.

Tobacco Jones said, "With her gone, a man can talk. Women clutter up things. The thing is simple, Bates. Somebody wants us killed. Them two killers figured we had empty shotguns. Doctored and useless ca'tridges."

Judge Bates nodded.

Tobacco Jones sipped coffee noisily. "It all adds up to that incident last night, when thet fellow tried to doctor our guns. Levis, goin' aroun' a corner, was all we saw."

"Which tell us nothing."

"Ree Helper, she wears levis."

"So do hundreds of other people on this range, Tobacco. Could have been Ree Helper; might not have been. Wish we could locate that gent that I sprinkled with beebees when we came into town, and we would know for sure who our enemies were, even if we didn't know why."

"Doc Goodenough is doctorin' him, I'd say." The lanky postmaster fingered his star. "I'm the law now. I'll send a deputy out to the Widder's place, whoever the Widder is and wherever her spread is."

"There'll be the right time and the right place," His Honor said, smiling. "You're the law now, Jones. Your duty is to dig down to the base of this trouble and settle it and drag the culprits before my court for trial."

"I dunno if I cotton to this sheriff deal, Bates."

"We came to sit on the bench for the remainder of the Helper trial," His Honor pointed out. "So far, we have had Miss Helper in our arms, but we haven't held her very long. You, as sheriff, are commissioned to find this woman, bring her into court."

"Quit your joshin', Bates. Here comes

the people with that other stiff what I shot."

"Go out and see if you recognize him."

Tobacco grumbled, got off the stool, and went outside. The sunshine was hot. Judge Bates looked at Lou, who had come out of the kitchen. Her face was flushed from heat and anger.

"Burned my roast, Judge!"

"Don't get burned up over it, girl."

She put her hands on the counter, palms down, and regarded him. His right hand went over her left.

"For a man who almost got killed, Judge Bates, you seem to have no fear. You joke like nothing happened — nothing at all."

"I'm still alive," His Honor pointed out. "You have a nice hand."

She looked around and said, "If people weren't watching, I'd hit you across the face just to be ornery! I don't trust you."

She pulled back her hand, for Mike Jacobs had entered. He waddled to a stool, slid onto it, looked at Bates. "Tough town, Your Honor. Maybe I'd best move on before I stop a bullet. I'm a pretty big man, and bullets are singing around here most of the time." His smile was tight. "What's behind all this?"

"You got me, Mr. Jacobs."

"I guess, to a certain degree, a judge is always in danger."

"Nothing new to me, Mr. Jacobs."

Lou took the man's breakfast order. Tobacco Jones and the others had the dead man on the stretcher. Tobacco waved for Judge Bates to come out. The judge had seen the dead man, but he did not know his name; he had seen him on the depot platform, too. But never in court.

"Take him into the morgue, and the inquest will be held tomorrow."

Tobacco said, "Be an inquest, no two ways about that — dead drummer, these two stiffs, an' the dead gink you shot the haid off'n, Bates."

"Get them all at once and clear the docket," His Honor said.

They carried the dead man away. His bronc also packed a brand alien to this section of Wyoming. The judge impounded both horses, intending to put them up for sale to pay the county the funeral expenses bound to be incurred while burying the two gunmen.

The livery-barn man — a bent over old fellow — led the broncs away at His Honor's orders.

Tobacco Jones bit off a chew, and the judge longingly thought of his jug in the hotel room.

Tobacco, his chew working, asked, "What's next, Bates?"

"You're the sheriff. Your sworn duty is to bring in Ree Helper."

"You goin' help me, Bates?"

"For you, yes, Jones. Hire some broncs at the livery barn. I'll get my jug and meet you there."

"See you, Bates."

The judge went to the hotel room. He stopped in to see Lawyer Weakspoon. The nurse was feeding the barrister. He lifted hate-filled eyes toward the judge.

"Just keep on your way," he snarled.

"When you get ready to talk, let me know."

"I kill my own lice, Bates."

"One almost killed you, Weakspoon. You got a gun handy?"

"Under my pillow."

"Keep it handy, lawyer. They might try it again. You know something that is valuable to me, but you'll tell me in time."

"I told you once and I repeat it: 'I kill my own lice'."

The judge spoke to the nurse. "Watch him night and day. Keep the door locked nights. Keep the windows locked down at all times and pull the blinds low at night. Remember that?"

"Yes, Your Honor."

Judge Bates looked at Jack Weakspoon. The attorney lay with closed eyes.

"Goodby, sir," he said.

He got his jug and walked toward the barn, thinking of Ree Helper.

11

REE HELPER protested, "I doctored their cartridges, like I said. They had real bullets in those shotguns when they shot down that pair of stooges of yours, Bart!"

Terry faced her, there in the Bucket of Suds.

"You sure you doctored them bullets, Ree?"

"You think I'm lying?"

Terry said, clipping his words, "Woman, what if John and I had called Bates and Jones, figuring they had empty guns — just like Spud and Killer figured? Bates and Jones would have killed us just like they downed Spud and Killer!"

"We might have got them," John Walker said tonelessly. "Spud and Killer whooped about being gunmen. When the showdown came, they didn't have too much speed."

"They figured they were going against men with useless guns," Terry pointed out. "They didn't need speed."

Ree Helper squinted out the window at Judge Bates. Her plan, she saw, had backfired. She had hoped that Terry and Walker would go against Judge Bates and Tobacco Jones. She had hoped to get rid of Bart Terry and John Walker.

"Wonder if those two knew that Spud and Killer worked for you?" she asked, looking at Terry.

"Nobody but us and Spud and Killer knew they worked for me," Terry pointed out. "I only hired them yesterday, and the hiring was not done in town, either. They said they were drifting south, and I caught them out on the range and hired them. I thought they were real gunslingers."

"If they were gunslingers," John Walker said, grinning tightly, "they're dead ones now, Terry."

Terry pounded a fist against the dressing table. "We're having too much tough luck! First, that holdup kicks back, now we send two men out to get rid of Bates and Jones. You know, there are four men in that morgue right now. And three of them are our hands!"

"Nobody can prove it," Walker pointed out.

Bart Terry stood motionless, listening to sounds from the saloon below him. Walker watched his boss, and Walker's thin face was expressionless. Ree Helper moved over and sat on the bed and said ironically, "Those girls of yours have soft jobs, Bart, judging from the softness of the mattress on this bed."

Bart Terry nodded absently. "That deed of yours should be cleared any day now, Ree, from what those lawyers tell me. When it is cleared, you'll own Thunder Canyon for sure, and the thing we want is ours."

"When the deed is clear and in my name, I cut you two in on it," Ree Helper said. "But there's another gent on this range that is dangerous to us, Bart."

John Walker looked at her.

Bart Terry nodded again. "Mike

Jacobs," he murmured. "Sent out by the railroad to buy right-of-way ahead of the rails, and then he tries to muscle in and cut out the company that hires him."

"No loyalty," Walker said cynically, jokingly.

"What about Mike Jacobs?" Ree Helper was persistent.

Bart Terry rubbed his soft hands together, and a cunning look entered his eyes. "If Jacobs hooks up with Bates and Jones, it could go rough on us. So far we've had some rough luck, but we've had some good luck, too. Nobody can pin any of those dead men on us."

"Mike Jacobs?" Ree Helper reminded him. "What do we do with him?"

Terry said, "Don't rub me, woman!" For a moment anger lighted his face. "Jacobs is a lawyer and he is smart. But he sort of likes a woman named Ree Helper, I notice."

Ree Helper smiled.

Terry said, "Jacobs was drinking here a few nights ago, with one of my girls. I tried to get her to pump him, but he kept his mouth shut, she told me. I guess he's on your hands, Ree . . . "

Ree Helper stood up, stretched her hands out in front of her.

"You going to get Jacobs, Ree?" Terry asked.

Ree spoke slowly, choosing her words. "I was the one that shot Weakspoon. I tried to kill him, but I shot too high . . . The point is this: what about you gents? I won't do it all."

"You got the upper hand," Terry pointed out, "because you're a woman. He'll eat out of your hand . . . but he sure won't eat out of mine. Lure him out to your homestead, and one of us will salt him down from the brush, savvy?"

"When?"

"As soon as you can get him out of town."

Ree Walker nodded. "Which one of you are going to do this little task, you nice little playmates?"

Terry's smile was thin, and his eyes were dead. "We'll talk that over later, honey."

154

Walker asked, "What about Bates and Jones?"

Terry turned, pivoting on a bootheel.

"They're only human, Terry. A bullet will kill them. So far, each sort of seems to bear a charmed life — we've missed two times. But we've never directly taken guns against them, man to man. And when that comes, we won't miss."

"In open gunfare?" Walker wanted to know.

Terry said, "Do I look like a fool, Walker?" He did not await an answer. "The brush is thick and a grave can never be found. And the brush hides a man and makes a murderous act an ambush act, savvy?"

"Good deal, Bart."

Terry said, "Go downstairs and watch from there, John."

John Walker looked at Ree Helper, said, "Okay, Bart." He went outside, and they stood there, a murderer and a would-be murderess, and they listened to him go down the stairway. Then Bart Terry looked at Ree Walker.

"Come here, honey."

She came toward him, and then her right hand flashed out, palm down, and she slapped him hard across the face.

"You vixen — "

She said quietly, "I'm not one of your paid workers, Bart. You can't order me around. When you talk to me, use kid gloves, and you'll get lots further."

He studied her, the mark of the slap plain on his face.

"I'm sorry, Ree."

She sat on the bed, smiling now. She had won her point; she had proven her power over this man.

"Bart, forgive me, please. I guess I'm upset. When we own Thunder Canyon for sure, when we get the rails through and the mines opened — Well, I'll be different, Bart. I promise that."

He said, "All right, Ree. Now work on Mike Jacobs Get him out of town into the badlands, and a bullet from either my gun or John's will do the rest."

"As soon as I can, Bart. Now let me rest, please. Keep the girl out of here for an hour or so while I sleep a little?"

He kissed her gently, stood up and said, "All right, Ree." He went to the door and stopped, looking back, one hand on the knob. "You won't be disturbed. Lock the door behind me."

She locked the door and leaned against it until she heard no sound from the hall. Then she unlocked the door again, went down the back stairway, stopped in the alley, looked around. She was hunted and she was wary. Within ten minutes, she stood in another room — this room, though, was in the hotel.

12

MIKE JACOBS had a cigar between his puffy lips. He looked at Ree Helper with speculative earnestness.

"Well, woman, what is it?"

Ree Helper said, "Thanks for inviting me to sit down." Her voice was ironic. She went across the room and took a chair and crossed her legs.

Jacobs rolled the cigar, his eyes hidden behind fat rolls.

"Well?" he asked again.

"I know your game, Jacobs. You're an attorney for the railroad. You heard about the copper in Thunder Canyon and that the rails have to go up that canyon. You hightailed out here to grab that canyon for yourself."

"Keep on talking."

"What's the use?" She shrugged. "I beat you to it. The canyon is mine, and you're on the outside looking in."

"The deed is not final."

"It will be in a day or so. You can't break a homestead because it's handed down by the fellow with the Long Whiskers, not the territory. The railroad has tried, you have tried — but neither of you can do it."

The cigar bobbed, the eyes were dull.

"Keep on talking, Miss Helper."

"I made a mistake."

"I know that."

"If you know so much, lawyer, what is the mistake?"

He regarded her steadily before slowly saying, "You needed help. You got it from two men. I won't say their names. You know them as well as I do. But now you're in the clutches of these two men."

"Who told you?"

The cigar moved as the thick lips moved. "I added one and one, and it didn't make three. Now, you want to break this triangle, and you've come to me."

"You're smart. I'm a dumb, ignorant woman."

He corrected her with evenly spaced words. "You're not dumb and ignorant. You're scheming and mean, Ree Helper."

"I won't get mad. I need your help too bad."

He took the cigar between thick fingers and regarded its gray tip. "This is hardly any place for us to talk. Terry and Walker are watching you like a cat watches a pail of milk. They'll look for you and find you in my room — "

"How will they know I'm here?"

"You went through the lobby. The clerk saw you."

She said, "That's right." That thought was not new to her. "Where can we talk, Mr. Jacobs?"

He stood up, and the cigar went into the spittoon. He came over and put his hands on her shoulders.

"Mike is the name."

"Mike, then."

"We can whip this whole bunch, Ree. You and I, working together."

"Yes."

He tried to kiss her, and she slid under

his arms and moved away. Anger had its way with him, flushing his porkish jowls, and she said, "Tomorrow, out by my homestead. Nobody can see us out there."

He stopped, and the anger receded. "Tomorrow afternoon," he said.

She agreed, "Tomorrow afternoon."

He watched her leave. She went down the back stairway into the alley. She was wanted and Engstrand was after her, and now Tobacco Jones was sheriff. She went down the alley and came into Terry's office by the back door. Terry had his boots on the desk and he was cleaning his six-shooter.

She said, "Mike Jacobs."

Sunlight came through the window to reflect on the six-shooter. "When?"

"Tomorrow afternoon. At Thunder Canyon."

The loading gate snapped closed. "John Walker," Terry said.

"Walker does it all. He says he'll get Weakspoon."

Terry's lips moved, and he said, "Why

pitch for Walker? You in love with the stiff?"

"Why do you say that?"

Terry said, "Walker, tomorrow, in Thunder Canyon. Maybe I'll take care of Weakspoon."

"That's the deal," she said.

The front door opened. Walker came in, and surprise touched him on seeing Ree Helper. "Bates and Jones just rode by the front, Bart. Heading toward Thunder. They'll head for your cabin, Ree."

"Nothing there, Walker."

Walker said to Terry, "Maybe we should trail them, Bart?"

Terry shook his head.

"Why not?"

"This is a good time to get Weakspoon. You could get Doc Goodenough into town. He's dead drunk, and he'd never know who shot through the window when he took care of Weakspoon."

"Goodenough is in town now. Just rode in."

Terry looked at Walker and did not see him. You killed one, then you had to kill another. And what about Goodenough — would he talk? One killing led to another, and finally you either won or somebody killed you ...

"Get him down to see Weakspoon. Tell him to get the nurse to leave on an errand. Weakspoon's room is next to the alley. The silencer is in my desk." He pulled open the tray.

"What about Goodenough, Bart?"

Terry played ignorant. "What do you mean?"

"Doc knows a lot. He's a drunk and he could talk. His words could get the law to put us behind bars for life. Or he could hang us."

"Right."

Walker looked at his cigaret and waited. Ree Helper stood and watched each man. A fly buzzed against the pane, a prisoner who wanted freedom.

"Do your best, Walker."

Walker looked at Ree Helper. Terry did not see her slowly shake her head. Walker said to Terry, "You do it, Bart. I'll take Jacobs."

"What's wrong with you?"

"I'll take Mike Jacobs," Walker said, and left.

Terry leaned back and his eyes went to Ree Helper. "Get out of here, and stay out for a while. Trail Bates and Jones."

"You sound rough. Don't order me — "

Terry got to his feet and went toward her and said, "I was only joking. You can stay as long as you want — we got the side room — "

"Now you *have* scared me!"

She went to the door, then slipped outside. Again, she looked up and down the alley, saw nobody. She went between two buildings, coming to another street, and she darted across this, reaching the willows along the creek. There was the smell of ferns and water, of trout and suckers, and a horse standing in the brush, tied to a cottonwood tree. She went into saddle and thumbed her nose in the general direction of Bart Terry and John Walker.

"Two fools," she told the horse. "Two

164

suckers for a woman's smile. May you roast in Hades."

The horse was long-legged and tough-gaited, and she rode the high ridges, the range moving out below her with its coulees and draws running off in the distance. When Kirby Helper had hooked up with her, the trouble had started — everything Kirby Helper had touched had turned vile and rotten. They had all got into the act, then, and now, one by one, they were being eliminated.

And that was good.

The dirty, cheap, scheming devils.

But what am I but cheap and scheming?

She looked over the rolling miles of endless country. The badlands have lots of rooms for graves, she thought cynically.

Gradually the country grew rougher, for she was nearing Thunder Canyon. To the west the mountains made a strong outline, a challenge to the rails that would soon seek to pierce their majestic silence.

An eagle circled, its shadow running across the pines and spruce.

You're free, eagle.

Then Thunder Canyon lay below her, falling out from under the hoofs of her bronc, boulders and rocks and pine and spruce. Along its bottom ran Thunder Creek, which, from this altitude, looked like a ribbon of gray strung out along the greenery of the timber and brush.

The canyon widened suddenly, becoming about half a mile wide at one point, then tapering off to become narrow again. The flat covered an area about five miles long, and the copper ledge was in the south side of the mountain, almost to the surface. Strip mining would uncover it.

Already, a man was at her cabin, and she dismounted and put her bronc in the buckbrush. She had field glasses and she watched the man.

He was Judge Lemanuel Bates.

She saw no sign of Tobacco Jones. She got the impression he was in the brush, a guard posted against possible trouble. These two were taking no chances, she saw, and this caused her to frown. She had hoped to run this pair against Walker and Terry and thus eliminate all who fell, but Terry had turned the tables.

Another bad stroke of luck.

Her glasses held Judge Bates. The jurist went into the cabin, walking with his rolling gait. She never locked the cabin. No use in locking a door when a window can be broken with the back of a man's hand or a rock. She let her glasses go across the brush surrounding the cabin. She and Kirby Helper, in order to hold their homestead rights, had plowed about ten acres, for the government demanded improvements, or the homestead entry would have been cancelled. This was brown with stubble, for heat had killed the wheat soon after it had sprouted.

She looked carefully, jaws tight behind the field glasses, but she saw no sign of Tobacco Jones, as she searched the brush.

Finally Judge Bates came out. He stood for a while in the yard, then went into the barn, a log affair with a brush roof. He was not long there; he came out and went into the high brush. She lost him and then found him again and again lost him. About ten minutes later, two riders, riding at a walk, came out of the timber, there at the far end of the mesa. They found the trail and put their broncs against the incline of the hill, seeking the top of the canyon. Judge Bates had joined Tobacco Jones and they were leaving Thunder Canyon.

What had they found?

"Nothing," she said aloud. "This girl is no fool, Bates. She leaves no evidence lying around for strange eyes to read."

She went down into the canyon, leading her horse, following a trail only she knew. Judge Bates and Tobacco Jones continued riding toward Muletown. His Honor rode deep in saddle, belly bouncing with each jogging step of his bronc.

"She's smart, Tobacco."

"Like all women. Like Lou. Like Imogene Carter."

"She left nothing open in the cabin, Tobacco."

"I figgered that, Bates."

His Honor untied his jug. "Drink?"

"You trying to joke with me, Lem?"

The judge drank and lowered the jug. "Hate to drink alone, friend. Well, we found nothing at the cabin to point to the cause of this trouble. I'd like to kill the territorial attorney for sicking me onto this case ice cold."

"One lawyer gypping another! That's good!"

The judge said, "Not professional ethics."

Tobacco bit off a chew. "I forgot I was sheriff for a while. Bates, I don't want the job."

"You got it anyhow."

Tobacco spat on a clump of bunchgrass. "I could watch that cabin, Bates. She'll come to it sooner or later and I can nab her."

"But could you hang onto her?" Judge Bates smiled slowly.

"What about this Doc Goodenough?

169

So he ain't out to the Widder's, they tell me. Where is he?"

"Doctorin' thet gent you winged."

"Where is that gent at?"

"Darned if I know. If Doc would show up we could pump him. Yonder comes a rider hell bent for election! Looks to me like it's a woman, Bates."

It was a woman.

Evidently Imogene Carter had left town in a hurry, for she had not even donned a riding-skirt.

"I thought you two might have ridden in this direction."

Judge Bates lifted his eyes to the woman's flushed face. She was rather pretty and had plenty of appeal.

"Why, Miss Carter, what is it?"

She told them in a few hurried sentences. Somebody had sneaked down the alley and had tried to kill Lawyer Weakspoon by shooting through the window. The room had been dark and the lawyer had not been hit. Instead, Doc Goodenough had been shot and killed.

"Goodenough? He in town, at last?"

His Honor asked.

"He had to be in town," she said, "or how the devil would he have got killed?"

"Did they catch the ambusher?"

"No. Nobody even saw him, in fact."

"Did the bullet miss Weakspoon?"

"Weakspoon wasn't in the room."

Judge Bates looked at Tobacco Jones, who had resumed masticating his cud. "Somebody tried to kill Weakspoon again. Instead, because of the darkened interior of the room, they got the doc, and rolled him over into the Happy Hunting Ground." He swung his sad eyes back to Imogene. "Where was Weakspoon?"

Again, rapid words. The nurse had gone out for something to eat. Doc. Goodenough, drunk as a hoot-owl, had gone to Weakspoon's room to take the nurse's place.

"Where was Weakspoon?" His Honor again asked.

"I'm getting to that. Nobody seems to have heard the rifle shot or pistol shot, whichever it was."

"Silencer. Where was Weakspoon?"

Anger touched her cheeks and gave her eyes a slanting savagery. "Weakspoon had apparently got out of bed and left, Your Honor. Nobody knows where he is. His horse is gone from the barn."

Judge Bates nodded. "Feared for his life, figuring maybe Doc Goodenough would kill him, or for some other reason — so he fled. And he is a wounded and sick man, too. Thanks, Miss Carter."

She turned her horse. "Thought you'd want to know."

"Good day, Miss Carter."

She looked at him. "Aren't you going back to town with me, Judge Bates?"

"No, Miss Carter."

She frowned, and her eyes found Tobacco Jones, who had a dumb look on his wide face.

"Where are you two going?"

"That," said Judge Bates, "is our business, Miss Carter."

"I'm quitting as your secretary!" she stormed.

"Think it over, Miss Carter."

"Men! You try to help them and you get no thanks!"

Her horse kicked back dust. Judge Bates leaned forward in the saddle and laughed. But the jaws of Tobacco Jones were stern and his cud, for once, was forgotten. He watched the judge and said nothing.

The judge said, "She was hopping mad."

"You didn't treat her too courteously, Bates."

"A knight of the old school. A tobacco-chewing, non-drinking knight of the Round Table."

"No place or time to joke, Bates."

"What's on your mind?"

"We cain't hightail back to town, Bates. This is ambush country and maybe we're marked next for the meat block."

"We been marked ever since that train holdup," His Honor pointed out. "That's nothing new added, Jones. You got eating tobacco enough?"

"An extra plug in my saddlebag, along

173

with some jerky and salt. And your jug?"

"Filled it afore I left town."

"We don't go into town, then?"

Judge Bates shook his head. "We sure don't. I can't imagine Weakspoon navigating far with that hole in his side. If we find him, he might tell us something."

"We might find him, and he might talk."

But they didn't find Weakspoon. They made camp that night in the brush high on the wall of Thunder Canyon. They talked it over. Ree Helper held the key to something, whatever it was, and they would watch her. The whole thing centered around the woman with the levi pants. The night was chilly, for snow was always on the western mountains, and dawn came slowly. When forenoon came they scouted the Terry ranch. From a ridge they watched the spread.

The outfit lay along the gradual slope of a long hill, nestling into the landscape and the dried grass. The house was high on the hill, a long building made of logs, the logs now gray and mostly covered with wild morning-glory vines. There was the bunkhouse and then the barn and the corrals, strung along the hillside, their bars made of cottonwood and pine stringers.

Tobacco said, "Guard over there in that bunch of brush, Bates." His field glasses went in a circle. "No other guard, though, thet I kin see. You see any?"

"Just the one."

"Nice-looking outerfit," Tobacco Jones said, and chewed his Horseshoe with methodical precision. "But we'd best get our rumps back to Thunder Canyon, eh?"

"Good idea."

13

BUT nobody was at the Helper house. They watched from the brush for a few minutes, saw nobody in the yard; no smoke came from the stovepipe chimney. And impatience showed in the thick face of Judge Lemanuel Bates.

"We ride toward town," he decided.

"Nothin' here," Tobacco Jones grunted.

They were almost to Muletown when Tobacco Jones said, "Rider leaving town, Bates, and it looks like this gink called Mike Jacobs."

The rider was ahead and below them, for they were coming down off the rimrock ledge. Judge Bates used his field glasses to make identification certain.

"That is he."

"Where is he going?"

Judge Bates tied his field glasses onto his saddle and untied his jug. He drank and said, "Damn if I know. But he is in this. He's about the only one what ain't been shot at or killed, eh, Jones?"

"He's takin' the trail to the Helper outerfit, Bates."

"Another of Ree's admirers maybe?"

They watched Mike Jacobs head toward Thunder Canyon. He rode as if he had a ton of bricks under his pants. He bounced along, killing himself and his horse. He probably suffered even more than the horse.

He found the trail leading down into the canyon and he walked down this, leading his horse. Plainly he did not trust his bronc on such a slope. Once he skidded and he landed sitting down, a ludicrous figure in the shale and rock. He got up and brushed off his pants and continued downward, finally reaching the floor of the canyon at the point where it started to spread out to become the flat on which the Helper farm was located.

"He still ain't climbin' on that horse," Tobacco said, and grinned. "Bet he ain't got no skin on the inside of his laigs, Bates."

The man walked across the clearing, lumbering like a bear, and they heard him call, "Hello, the house."

"Prob'ly read that in some Western story," Judge Bates said. "Them writers don't know no more about the West than — Hello, Jones, look! Somebody's been in that house all the time, and we watched it and saw nothing."

"Ree Helper, Bates."

High on the rim of the canyon another man watched as he squatted in the shadow of a big sandstone boulder with the shadow hiding him. He watched Ree Helper walk out to meet Mike Jacobs. This man wet his thumb and tested the wind and he arranged the sight on his Winchester .30–30. His face was mean and ugly and his eyes were small and strong on the pair below.

This man did not see Bates and Jones.

Neither did the judge or his partner see John Walker.

The partners watched the two people below them there on the floor of the canyon. John Walker watched these two people, too. The partners watched with interest, heightened by curiosity; the interest of John Walker held also jealousy. His fingers were strong against the worn stock of the Winchester.

Tobacco Jones watched through his field-glasses.

Slower and slower his jaws moved as he chewed. Finally he stopped chewing altogether, his mouth opened slightly.

"She's kissin' him, Bates," Tobacco grunted. He resumed chewing. "Love . . . for a purpose. A woman can make a sucker outa any man she wants."

"Sometimes."

"*All* the time."

His Honor said no more on that point. Tobacco Jones had made up his mind, and his judgment, in his own estimation, was always correct. Judge Bates watched the pair below. He smiled in amusement.

Jacobs, he decided, was a supreme

fool. What good-looking girl would fall for such a pot-bellied guy? The judge looked down at his own belt. He *was* getting a little bit heavy, at that.

"Look at 'em now, Bates."

Ree Helper seemed very, very happy. She had Mike Jacobs by the hand, school kid fashion, and her other arm was swinging happily as they went toward the cabin. Then they were inside the farmhouse.

The judge looked at his watch.

This done, he studied the canyon, wondering what all the trouble was about. This canyon looked worthless. Brush-coated walls, rocks and boulders, with a bit of farmland below.

"What would you do with this canyon, Tobacco?"

"I don't own it, Bates."

"Well, saying you did own it — what good would it be to you?"

"Run goats on. I doubt if a goat could find a living on these slopes, though. Besides, he might fall off an' bust a leg."

"That railroad into Muletown is right bumpy," Judge Bates said quietly. "The rails end there, and by rights they should go over the Rockies and into Salt Lake and then to the Coast."

"Yeah, that's right."

"This might be the pass the railroad company wants. Right through this canyon, Jones."

"Jes' guesswork. How long they been in that cabin?"

The judge dug out his watch. "About ten minutes. There she comes out of the house."

Tobacco focused his glasses. "I must be loco. She's carryin' her shirt."

"That's right."

Ree Helper went to an upright pole beside the barn. She pulled on a rope and her shirt went up in the air. It hung limply.

"She must've washed her shirt," Tobacco said.

"That," said His Honor, "is a signal to somebody. She might have made the pretense of washing her shirt, but what a heck of a clothesline that is — like a flagpole."

"Who could she be signalin'?"

The judge said nothing but he searched the canyon wall with his glasses. Tobacco watched Ree Helper go back into the house. Then, when the door was shut behind her, he let loose a huge sigh. And he looked at his partner.

"See anybody, Bates?"

"Yes, I do. Over by those boulders across the canyon. See that man crouched there, with a rifle?"

"I don't see — Yes, I do. By heck, it was a signal, like you said! Who is that gent?"

"You recognize him?"

Tobacco looked long and hard and finally said, "Looks like John Walker, Bates. What say you?"

"John Walker, I'd say."

"Ambush rifles, Bates?"

"Might be."

Another few minutes passed, and then Ree Helper and Mike Jacobs came out of the cabin. Hand in hand, they went along the far slope of the mountain, stopping occasionally. Gradually they worked their way toward a spot below the hidden rifleman. They stopped and studied the ground.

"What they lookin' for, Bates?"

"Looks to me like they're checking the location stakes of her homestead. They must want to make sure it covers a certain area of ground. Or so it appears to me, Jones."

"She's workin' him over so he'll be closer to John Walker. Bates, they aim to murder that man."

"What can we do? The distance is so far we couldn't hope to send a rifle ball over around Walker to scare him. We just got to sit here and watch."

"Sure will be tough."

The judge, "We're unable to help."

"Maybe we read this wrong," Tobacco Jones said.

By this time Jacobs and Ree Helper were quite a distance away. Bates saw Mike Jacobs climb onto a big boulder, apparently seeking height so he could see

183

his surroundings better. For a moment the heavy-set man stood poised with Ree below him, the boulder between her and John Walker.

Judge Bates said, "Here it goes, Jones."

John Walker shot three times. Because of the distance, the reports were hardly audible, but they saw the puff of smoke from his rifle. The second bullet hit Mike Jacobs and he started to fall. The third straightened him momentarily and he slid off the rock, limp and huge. He hit the ground and lay still, almost at the feet of Ree Helper, who had fallen to the ground behind the rock, safe from the bullets of John Walker.

Ree Helper straightened and went over to where Mike Jacobs lay, and she knelt beside the man for some time.

"Checking as to his present state of health," Judge Bates said.

"Terrible thing to say about a man, Bates."

The judge said, "Maybe he murdered somebody in his time, Tobacco. Even innocent Doc Goodenough got killed, you know."

"Mebbe he wasn't so innercent, Bates."

Her inspection finished, Ree Helper climbed onto the boulder and waved her hands over her head. Walker then pulled back into the rocks and disappeared.

"Bates, he's pulled stakes!"

"Probably going back to report to Bart Terry. I'm going up and see if I can get any altitude and still see Walker."

"If I had a gal thet purty waitin' for me, dead man or no dead man, I'd pay her a long visit."

"She's Terry's woman, remember? And Terry might not like to have Walker around his woman!"

"Terry's, bah! Anybody's woman."

The judge had no appetite for further discussion along this line, and he circled higher up on the wall of the canyon, at last coming to the rim. From here he saw two riders heading across country toward the Terry spread. His hunch had been correct. While John Walker had ambushed Mike Jacobs, Bart Terry had waited for his henchman back over the rim of the canyon. Now both were heading for the Terry spread. They went into a gully and out of sight, and Judge Bates slid down the slope and hunkered beside Tobacco Jones.

"Somebody waited for him. Figure it was Bart Terry."

"Wonder why they didn't come down and check on the dead gent with Ree Helper, 'stead of leaving her alone to bury that dead man? And he must be dead, 'cause he sure ain't sittin' up."

"He's dead, all right. Her signal from the top of the rock told Walker that."

"Then why didn't they ride down?"

"Might not want to be seen too much with her. Besides, let somebody ride up unexpectedly, and here is the great Walker and Terry, with a dead man — an ambush is a terrible crime, Jones."

"They aim to lay it all on the girl, eh?"

"That looks like it."

"What do we do now?"

The judge searched every bit of the

terrain with his glasses before answering. Finally he lowered the glasses with, "We ride down there, Tobacco. We come in behind the shack, leave our broncs there, and then we have a nice talk with one Ree Helper."

"Hope she leaves her shirt off." Tobacco grinned.

They got down the canyon and came in from behind the cabin there in the clearing. Ree Helper had come back for a shovel and was at the scene of the ambush, digging in the soft dirt of the plowed field, when they halted in the brush and watched her.

Both Bates and Jones carried their catch-ropes. Judge Bates smiled and glanced at Tobacco and said, "She still wears no shirt, friend."

"Buryin' a dead man, eh?"

"She was burying Kirby Helper, remember, when they caught her and held her for trial."

"Now we'll catch her!"

They came out of the brush, ropes built into loops. Ree heard them for the first time and she turned, holding the shovel. Judge Bates saw the surprised look on her tanned face. It was more than a surprised look; it was a *stunned* look . . .

"What in the — ?"

She dropped the shovel. She turned to run. She started out with antelope swiftness, a startled wildling.

"Rope her, Jones!"

Her rifle leaned against a boulder about fifty feet away.

"Don't let her git thet Winchester, Bates!"

His Honor's loop went out, singing through the air. He sent the rope out too far, and he jerked it back, hoping to settle it around her shoulders. But she ducked, and his loop fell harmlessly and empty to the ground.

They had to keep her from reaching that Winchester!

Suddenly she went down. Tobacco Jones had laid his loop out ahead of her, and although she had jumped to avoid it he had maneuvered it so she had got both legs in it.

He hauled back hard, and kept her down. She cursed and tried to kick the rope off, sitting down as she worked, but he dragged her on her rump, keeping the rope tight.

"Done caught me a filly, Bates."

"Let go of me — "

The judge had her rifle. Tobacco let slack go into the rope. He grinned. The girl got to her feet, and her anger had changed to blazing fury.

"You two bit woman-hating fools! What has got over you two, anyway?"

"We want to talk to you," Judge Bates said.

She was slapping her shapely derriere, and dust flew out of her levis.

"What about?"

"Well, this dead man here, for one thing."

"I found him dead here. I was burying him in a shallow grave before going to town to notify this so-called sheriff here!" She had only scorn for Tobacco Jones.

"Who killed him?" the judge asked.

"I don't know. I found him there — dead. He's been shot."

The judge looked at her. "You killed him. We saw you ambush him."

"You lie, and you know it."

She was biting her bottom lip hard. She studied him, and he knew this calmness was only a cloak to hide her raw nerves. She was brainy, and could be cool and tough when the occasion demanded.

The judge looked at Tobacco Jones' long hangdog face. Tobacco apparently was going to let him do all the talking.

"We saw you kill him."

"You must have been drunk if you saw me kill him. That rifle of mine over there is a .25-20, and a .30-30 killed this gent — "

"How do you know?"

For a moment, she seemed trapped. She did not look at either of them.

"I could tell by the size of the bullet holes in him."

Her quick wits had taken her out of a precarious situation. The judge grudgingly had silently to admit that point.

"If you didn't kill him, Miss Helper, who did?"

"I thought you said you saw me kill him?"

The judge laid down the law in no uncertain terms. "I'm asking the questions here, young lady, and you're answering them. We know you didn't kill him. We saw the ambusher shoot him from the rimrock. But you lured him onto this rock so the murderer could line him clearly on his sights. That makes you an accomplice to murder, and *murder* is a dirty little six-letter word, woman. If you talk things will go easier with you. We know who is in this mess, too."

"If you know so much, then why ask me?"

The judge tried a new angle.

"Sister, we're taking you to Muletown, and into a cell you go. And we're deliberately leaving you unguarded to see what happens."

"They killed Doc Goodenough,"

Tobacco Jones said. "They shot at Weakspoon when he was in the clink. They wounded Weakspoon. They'll prob'ly kill you."

A voice came from the brush behind them. "They won't kill her!"

14

FOR a moment there was silence. Judge Bates was surprised, and his heavy face showed this. Tobacco Jones' mouth was open. Ree Helper stood silent, fear on her pretty face. None of them had heard the speaker advance through the brush.

They turned.

Tobacco Jones, on recognizing the speaker, clicked shut his jaws, the sound of his teeth audible. Ree Helper stared, fear still on her. Her gaze was riveted on the rifle held by the speaker.

Judge Bates was the first to speak, "What kind of a deal is this, Weakspoon?"

The lawyer looked like a hunted animal. Gone was the courtroom sleekness, the marks of education, the veneer of civilization. His shirt hung in torn ugliness about his naked torso, stuck in his belt, and the bandage around his belly, right above the belt, was caked and stiff with dried blood. He had come through the buckbrush, and few twigs and leaves were embedded in his matted hair.

But it was his eyes and his mouth that attracted Judge Lemanuel Bates.

They were the eyes and the mouth of a wounded, trapped animal.

The eyes were glistening, high with fever, bright with hate. The mouth opened and closed, saliva drooling from the corners, the whiskers thick and stiff around the mouth and on the jowls.

The lawyer held a Winchester rifle. He clung to it, hands gripping it, fingers talons on it. He was dying on his feet, and his eyes and mouth showed this. Yet in his eyes glistened something beside insanity. Fear? Hope? Terror? Revenge?

Judge Bates settled for the last-named.

"Weakspoon, what do you want?" His Honor made his voice savage and hard. He still held Ree Helper's rifle. "Come on, man; talk, and make it fast. You're out on your feet!"

The jaws worked, saliva drooled. The eyes, hot with fever, flicked to His Honor, dwelled on him momentarily, then moved to Tobacco Jones, who was inching toward his right.

"Stay right where you are, Jones! You're not jumping me from the side. I'd kill you and not blink an eye. I'm a dead man as it is, and I don't give a darn if you beat me to Boothill or not!"

Tobacco Jones said, as calmly as he could, "I hold no grudge against you, Weakspoon."

"Just stay where you are!"

The rifle gestured, the movement demanding. Tobacco Jones froze and watched the lawyer with vigilant alertness.

Ree Helper said, "Let me help you, Jack. I can dress your wound — "

"Stay back there, darn you! I came to kill you, Ree! You don't know this, but I glimpsed you the night you ambushed me in that cell. I woke up in time to catch a look at you, you ambushing hussy!"

"You lie, Jack!"

Ree Helper screamed her words. Jack

Weakspoon screamed something — a wild and highpitched animal scream — and Ree Helper stood still as the bullets hit her. The lawyer shot twice. The first bullet hit the woman in the belly, right below her ribs, and the second caught her in the arm, breaking her right arm below the elbow. By this time, Judge Bates was shooting.

He shot three times, hitting Weakspoon each time. His Honor did not have time to aim. He shot as he raised the rifle, and he shot with deliberate accuracy. He had to kill this man, or the demented attorney would kill him and Tobacco Jones. It was self-defense.

Then it was all over.

Ree Helper was on the ground, sobbing and gasping. She lay on her side, and blood stained the earth. Weakspoon had staggered back and had dropped his rifle. He sat now at the base of a sandstone rock, staring at the body of Mike Jacobs.

"I'll be with you soon, Mike," he said.

Judge Bates said, "Tend to the girl,

Tobacco," and knelt beside Weakspoon. He said, "I hated to shoot you, Jack."

The whiskery face showed a thin smile. "That's all right, Bates. You didn't kill me. I'd have died from that hussy's bullet. I just — kept on my — feet long enough. Lord, I'm tired."

"Where do Terry and Walker come into this, Jack?"

"You don't know?"

"I asked you, Jack."

Weakspoon looked at Tobacco Jones. "Is she dead, Jones?"

"She is."

Weakspoon said, "Now I can die in peace. I'll meet you over the Ridge, you beautiful little devil."

His head went down and he stopped breathing. He went to one side, and Judge Bates let him sag to the ground. Then His Honor went over to where Tobacco knelt beside Ree Helper.

"Is she dead, like you said?"

"I lied to him, Bates, thinking he might tell us something, if he was sure that Ree was dead. He loved the woman,

197

and with her alive he might hold back to pertect her."

"Get her on her back, Jones."

They got the woman on her back. Evidently she had passed out from the shock and pain. Tobacco got his hat and went to Thunder Creek and came back with some water. He had also soaked his bandana in the creek. Judge Bates said, "Give me some of your eating tobacco, Jones."

"You takin' the habit, friend?"

Judge Bates bit off a chew. He grimaced, said, "Tastes like chewing poisoned oak to me, although I'm not in the habit of chewing poisoned oak. Clean the wound good, friend."

Carefully Tobacco sponged the blood away from the hole in Ree Helper's belly. The hard-jacketed bullet had made but a small blue hole, and the hole where the bullet had come out was no bigger than where it entered because of the steel jacket. Had the attorney shot her with a soft-nosed slug he would have torn out her intestines.

The girl breathed deeply, bosom rising and falling. Color was returning to her face. With the blood washed away from the wound in front, it did not look so deadly as it had at first. Judge Bates carefully wadded up some of the tobacco he had softened by chewing. With a turning movement, he forced this wad into the wound, sealing it.

"Now, if she doesn't bleed internally, we might be able to get her to town. Tough Doc Goodenough got killed."

"We'll roll her on her side, eh?"

"That's right."

With Ree Helper on her side, they washed the girl's back, laying bare the point where the bullet had made its departure. This wound was also plugged with tobacco by the judge.

"How about her arm?"

The judge tested the arm. It hung freely and he heard bones grate. "Broken," he said. "Get some dry wood from along the creek, and we'll make splints and make no effort to set the bone."

"Be best, Bates."

When Tobacco Jones returned, Judge Lemanuel Bates had maneuvered Ree Helper around so she sat with her back against a sandstone rock. The judge had taken off his shirt and put it between her bare back and the rock so the rock's surface would not scratch her skin. The girl had also regained consciousness. When her eyes opened the first thing she had seen had been the body of Lawyer Jack Weakspoon.

"You killed him, Judge?"

"Yes, Miss Ree. Much as I hated to kill a fellow human — "

"He was no good. The no account son of a good father. Am I going to die, Judge?"

"I don't know."

"I don't think so. Not this time, anyway. I'll bet you're wondering what all this fighting and scrapping is over, aren't you?"

"I am."

"Then you just keep on wondering, Judge. Because I'm not telling you a thing until I get a good lawyer."

Judge Bates kept his face blank. This woman was a tough nut, no two ways about that.

"I'll be the judge at your trial, Miss Ree. If you tell me now, I promise things will go easier with you."

She looked at him. She looked at Tobacco Jones. She smiled a little, and pain was in her smile, but amusement was there also.

"A woman — a pretty woman — is a hard animal to convict, Judge. I can lie like a house on fire, and the jury will believe me because I'm a pretty woman. As for you and Jones, you can both go straight to blazes!"

Her lips tightened in pain, and she grimaced. By this time the partners had her arm bandaged and in a makeshift sling. Judge Bates looked at Tobacco Jones. The Cowtrail postmaster chewed tobacco slowly.

"Nice young woman," Tobacco Jones murmured.

Judge Bates stood up and looked around. The scene was not too appetizing. Two dead men — Weakspoon, sprawled across the soil, mouth agape; Mike Jacobs, big and flabby and very, very dead. And maybe a rifle-man on the rimrock looking down on them.

They had to chance that.

"What's the deal?" Tobacco Jones asked. "We gotta git this heifer into town for a bed and care from the nurse, Bates. Me an' you have only nursed cows an hosses, not women."

"She isn't going to town, Jones."

"Why not?"

"Don't think she could stand a trip that long in her condition. She's lost lots of blood, and she might die before we got her to Muletown."

"Then where can we take her?"

"To the nearest ranch."

Tobacco said, "That means we'll take her to the Terry ranch."

Ree Helper said, "I'm not going to Bart Terry's outfit. I hate the dirty devil."

"You kissed him, remember?" the judge reminded her.

She looked at His Honor. "You talk

like a locoed jackass, Judge. I never kissed that skunk of a Bart Terry in my life. Explain yourself."

Despite her misery, she was alert and watchful.

"I saw you kiss him one night in the alley down in Muletown. Right after that, somebody knocked me cold. I know that Terry didn't knock me cold because he was too busy with you."

"You saw that?"

"Then you admit it?"

"I admit nothing. Your eyes are bad. I'm not going to the Terry ranch, and that is final."

"You go where we take you, young lady."

"But not to the Terry ranch."

"Why not?"

"I don't want to go there."

The judge said, "Tobacco, go up to your bronc on the hill and head for the Terry spread. Come back with some men and a stretcher and a bed in a wagon so we can transport this girl."

"All right, Judge."

When Tobacco had left, His Honor sat beside Ree Helper, his back to the rock.

"When you get stronger, we'll move you to town."

"I don't want to go there, Judge."

"Why? You worked with Walker. We saw him shoot down Mike Jacobs. You and Walker and Terry are old friends, I take it. You kissed Terry long and lovingly. You helped Walker kill Jacobs."

"Those two — they'll murder me — "

"They are solid substantial citizens," His Honor said in make-believe sincerity. "Walker now — he'd never kill anybody — in the open. You'll not be harmed, girl. I'll make that ranch a military reservation and, if necessary, will get the militia out to protect you."

"Can you do that?"

"I'm a federal judge, remember."

"I'm going to die," Ree Helper said in a low sick voice.

They sat there in silence. Her head came down and rested on Judge Bates' wide and fatherly shoulder. The jurist felt only sympathy and sorrow for this unfortunate woman, the same sorrow and sympathy he had for any misguided and weak person. She became very quiet, her breathing low. A fly buzzed over the face of the dead Weakspoon. The judge wanted to cover the lawyer's thin face with a bit of the barrister's torn shirt, but he did not dare move because of Ree's weight on his shoulder. So the fly buzzed and buzzed.

Ree Helper asked, "When is Jones coming back?"

"He should be back any time."

"I wish he'd hurry."

The judge spoke kindly. "Why don't you talk to me, Ree, and tell me all about this trouble? I promise it'll help you when we get these killers into court."

"You'll never get them into court."

"Why not?"

"You'll have to kill them first. They'll fight until they die. Walker is wanted for murder in New Mexico. In Texas, too."

"Did he tell you that?"

"He got drunk one night — I've said too much."

"They started out fighting you, remember?" Judge Bates selected his words with care. "Then they wanted your land because you were on Terry range. Then, when your husband got killed — "

"He wasn't my husband. We were divorced. But he trailed me here — saw a chance to cash in — "

She became silent. The fly buzzed industriously. Back in the pines a bluejay made his raucous, saucy calls. A muletail deer came out of the brush and grazed in the clearing about a hundred yards away. He was a four-point buck, and he saw them but paid no attention.

The buck grazed and browsed off the young cottonwood trees.

The judge prompted, "Cashed in on what?"

"I'd better keep my mouth shut."

And she would say nothing more, despite the judge's subtle promptings. He kept on asking her questions and she kept on refusing to answer. The only questions she would answer were those regarding her physical condition. She was as healthy as a young colt, and color came back to her cheekbones.

"How do you feel inside, Ree?"

"I'm not bleeding. But when they move me I might start again."

"We'll move you very carefully."

"Tobacco sure is gone a long time, it seems to me. Maybe he is taking the lower end of the canyon route. You can get in there with a rig, you know."

"I never knew that."

She had surmised correctly. Within ten minutes, they heard an approaching rig, and the buck deer bolted away on stiff legs into the brush and became lost from view. The rig turned out to be a spring wagon with a cot in the back, and with John Walker driving the team, Tobacco Jones on the seat beside him. Walker pulled the rig around, a bland look on his face, and said, "Trouble, eh?"

"Sure is," His Honor said. "Jacobs tried

to get tough with Ree here. Weakspoon was on the premises, it seems, and he killed Jacobs, but Jacobs got in some shots, too. In the mele, the girl got wounded."

John Walker nodded, still somber and calm. He looked at the dead Jacobs, and Judge Bates watched the killer's face as he looked down on a man he had murdered from the rimrock in dirty ambush.

"Dead as a mackerel," Walker said. He stirred Weakspoon's body with his toe. "This gent is a goner, too. *Rigor mortis* has already set in." He lifted his inscrutable eyes and looked at Judge Lemanuel Bates. "All over a skirt. Or should I say, over a woman not in a skirt, but in levis?"

"Your jokes," said Ree Helper weakly, "are sour, Walker. Like you are."

Walker said, "Oh, she's got a sense of humor, eh?"

Tobacco Jones was taking down a makeshift stretcher. "We made this at the Terry spread, and that took us some time. Got a blanket between two poles. How do you do this, Bates?"

They laid the stretcher on the ground and rolled the woman onto it, taking it slow and easy. Ree Helper gritted her teeth and kept from groaning. They got her on her back, and then they lifted the stretcher and laid her on the bed in the spring wagon.

"Just leave the stretcher under her," Judge Bates said. "We can unload her easy with her lying on it."

Walker said, "How about these dead stiffs?"

"Send somebody back from your spread to bury them."

"Where we taking this woman?"

"To the Terry outfit, your home spread."

Walker was on the seat, Tobacco sitting beside him. Walker had the reins in his hands and one boot on the brake.

"To the Terry spread?"

"Closest place, Mr. Walker. She can't be moved into town until she becomes stronger."

Walker considered that, not looking at Judge Bates. But His Honor, watching closely, thought he saw a gleam of satisfaction enter the killer's eyes.

"Reckon that's good logic."

Judge Bates looked at Tobacco Jones. "Be careful with her, Jones."

Tobacco nodded, understanding. Ree Helper was not to be alone with anybody for a moment. John Walker misread the statement entirely: he figured the judge was simply asking his partner to be very watchful of Ree Helper's welfare and comfort. Which was all right with Judge Lemanuel Bates.

"I'll take careful to driving her to the ranch," Walker assured them.

The spring wagon left at a slow gait, heading for the road that led upward out of Thunder Canyon. Judge Bates got the shovel and dug two shallow graves and temporarily buried Lawyer Jack Weakspoon and Mike Jacobs. This job done, he got his bronc and rode to the Helper ranch-house, where he diligently searched the spread again. He went over it with a fine-toothed comb and found nothing indicating why anybody would kill and rob for such a rocky and seemingly worthless place as Thunder Canyon.

He rode then toward the Terry spread. Bart Terry, so Tobacco had related, had ridden into Muletown, and Walker had been alone at the big spread. That made logic. Terry would keep a vigilant watch in Muletown while John Walker held down the same post at the Terry ranch.

These killers were smart.

They missed no angles, the devils.

He knew now for sure that John Walker and Bart Terry were behind these murders. But he did not know why they wanted Thunder Canyon. Ree Helper knew, but she would not tell.

His Honor did some thinking.

By the time he got to the Terry ranch, they had already taken Ree Helper from the springwagon, and she was in bed. The guard stopped His Honor and then had let him ride on unmolested.

When riding into the hoof-packed

211

yard, the judge's gaze did not miss a thing. His methodical memory had stored things accurately for possible future use. This, His Honor figured, would be the showdown.

15

LAMPLIGHT glistened on the blue-steel barrel of the Colts six-shooter. Long fingers turned the pistol, and facets of lamplight sparkled. The loading gate opened and the fingers turned the cylinder slowly. Dull brass cartridges were ugly in the lamplight.

"Well, I'll be darned," Bart Terry said.

"She's out at the ranch now," John Walker growled. "In bed, shot through the middle, with a arm busted. Shot by that shyster lawyer. I came into town to get the nurse out there. I wonder if them two saw me shoot down Mike Jacobs."

Cold fear rimmed the gunman's voice.

Bart Terry lifted his eyes from the six-shooter and looked at John Walker. "You sound as though you got ice in your boots, John."

"Well, if they saw me — They got the

213

deadwood on me, Bart. They'll take me back to New Mexico or Texas — and they'll hang me . . . "

Terry showed a thin smile. "They won't take you back to Texas or New Mexico to hang you," he promised. "If you get your neck stretched it'll be right here in Wyoming Territory, not in the southwest."

Walker snarled, "Nice company you are, Bart!"

Terry got to his feet and walked to the window. He stared at the lowered blind, and then he paced the floor. His bootheels made hollow sounds. From the saloon beyond his office came the sounds of men and women and the banging of the out-of-tune piano. The sounds seeped through the insulated wall and rubbed against the nerves of John Walker. They irritated Bart Terry, too, but his face did not show this.

"For Gawd's sake, Bart, quit that walkin' back an forth, please!"

Terry stopped, the six-shooter dangling from one finger. His smile spread across his face, but still it was hard. His lips moved slowly.

"You nervous, John?"

"Foolish question . . . What if this girl blabs to Bates and Jones about us? What if she tells them that I killed Judge Weakspoon? That you shot down Kirby Helper? What then, Terry?"

"She won't talk."

"Why do you say that?"

"She's in too deep. She's money-hungry and greedy as a human can get. She's tried to kill for Thunder Canyon — remember, she shot young Weakspoon, and the judge knows that. When a person gets to the point where he or she will commit murder, then that person won't talk. They'll lie in bed numb and with clenched lips."

"Don't forget that dead drummer, Bart. His blood is on our hands, too. That makes three they could get us for, and murder is a dirty charge — "

"Close your mouth. They'll hear you out in the saloon!"

John Walker studied his partner. "And

you said my nerves were shot!" He laughed with metallic hardness. "All right, Big Brain, she's your problem. And you'd better come up with the right answers, or this boy will grab a bronc and drift north to Canada!"

"You run out on me and I'll kill you!"

"Well, what's the deal?"

"Tell me more, John."

"I've repeated the story twice. What more is there to tell? Bates and Jones claim they can make our ranch a military reservation because Bates is a federal judge. They can keep us off our own property, Bates says."

Bart Terry nodded, deep in thought.

"Can they do that, Bart?"

"I don't know. I'm no lawyer. But I can tell you one thing, John. I'm going to let them do it. I'm not going to fight them."

"You're not going to fight them? Heck, Bart, they'll get us jugged, man!"

"You didn't let me finish. I'm not going to fight them — in the open.

From the brush, yes . . . "

John Walker smiled, but the smile was not pretty. "That's better. We got too much at stake here to take it on the run . . . This saloon, the ranch, and Thunder Canyon. But what if Ree Helper dies? Who gets Thunder Canyon then?"

"We do."

"We do? But the deed our lawyers is fixin' — it's in her name. How could we get it if she kicked the bucket?"

"She didn't read all the fine print." Bart Terry spun the cylinder of the .45. The ratchet made a fast series of clicking sounds. "The fine print says that if she dies the outfit goes to two men — John Walker and Bart Terry. Does that simplify things, John?"

Walker watched him. Walker's eyes were bright pinpoints of greed. His tongue moved out and wet his lips.

"Yes, it does, Bart."

"To what degree?"

Walker said slowly, "It makes a dead woman out of Ree Helper. I should have killed her when I shot down Mike Jacobs.

I aimed to, but she hid behind that rock. She's got brass and guts, that woman."

"But most of all, she's got greed."

"What's the first move?"

"Just bide our time."

"And hope she keeps her mug latched down tight?"

"That's it, John. We ride out to the ranch and look things over. Have you notified the nurse yet?"

"No."

"Then do it and meet me at the livery barn."

Walker grabbed Terry's arm. "If that nurse gets out there, Bart, how can we get in there and kill Ree, with the nurse watching?"

"We'll get around that. Just now the play is to act like we're co-operating with Bates and Jones. The badlands is a mighty big place, John, and a grave is a mighty small thing. And a bullet never cares who it kills."

"I don't know about this plan — "

"You don't have to know. Just do as I tell you. When we get Bates and Jones in the right position we kill them, and the badlands take over. A million men could search a million years and never find their graves in that wilderness."

"Well, all right . . . "

"Go get the nurse."

Walker went out into the saloon, and Terry picked up a rifle and jacked the breech open to verify its loads. Satisfied, he restored his .45 to its holster and went down the alley, carrying the Winchester. Thinking and scheming, Terry came to the livery barn. Already the nurse was there with John Walker. She was a big woman, always joking, heavy on her feet, with matronly front.

"You can't get me on a horse, however gentle. I'd break his back, I'm that heavy. You'll have to have a buckboard for me."

"You drive her out, Walker."

The lighted lantern, hanging from a rafter in the barn, showed Walker's displeasure. But the gunman said, "With pleasure, madam."

Terry led a sorrel out of a stall and

crammed a bit between grass-colored teeth. He smoothed out his saddle blanket, and his saddle came down and he tied the latigo tightly.

"See you at the ranch, Walker."

"You riding ahead?"

Terry mounted, a hard, tough bunch of muscle.

"At the ranch," he repeated, and turned the sorrel and hit him with his spurs. The bronc loped down the main street, then was on open range.

The wind, cooling the rangelands, was smooth against Bart Terry's face, touching his skin with light fingers. Sage filled the air with its clean odor, and the dust was good. He thought, We need rain, and then he smiled at this thought, for he was not worried about rain. He was worried about Judge Bates and a lanky postmaster named Tobacco Jones.

What if Ree Helper talks?

The sorrel, his first run gone, settled to a long trot. Bart Terry rode high on stirrups, palms flat on the fork of his saddle, bracing himself against the jarring gait of his horse.

What was Judge Bates doing and thinking?

At that moment, Judge Bates and Tobacco Jones were standing beside the bed that held Ree Helper. Lamplight glistened on the white pillow and showed the pale face of the woman. It hung in shadows across the craggy face of Tobacco Jones, and lost itself in the features of the judge.

"She's dead, Bates?"

"She just expired, Tobacco."

Tobacco Jones resumed chewing. He looked down at the pale face, and his voice was gentle.

"A tough way to end a life that once held great promise, Bates. A bullet through the belly from a crazed man she had tried to kill . . . What happens to people to make them step off into the deep?"

"When man knows all the answers to that question then he can abolish penitentiaries and jails. She did it for greed, I suppose. Most of them become criminals because they either do not want to work for what they desire, or they haven't the intelligence to get what they want."

Tobacco watched His Honor hit his jug for a long swallow. Then the jug came down, and the grim face of the jurist could be seen.

"She was our drawing card, a man might classify her . . . With her dead, there is no reason for Terry and Walker to sneak in to kill her, Bates."

"That's right."

"Bates, we've lost again. She died without telling us why they fought over Thunder Canyon. You have the theory that the railroad aims to run through the canyon to get over the Rockies, and she aimed to hold the land at a high price for right-of-way, seeing she had the railroad over the barrel."

"I still believe that, Jones. And my theory will not be hard to check on, either. Just one little telegram to the railroad headquarters in Omaha will tell us whether or not my guess is true."

"But there is more than that, Bates. Even if she had got a danged high price for the right-of-way, it wouldn't have paid off enough in dollars and cents to get her head danged near into a noose with a platform ready to drop out under her feet."

"We'll find out, Jones."

Again, Tobacco Jones chewed in thoughtful revery. "But we aimed to lure in them two killers, hopin' they would try to murder her to shut her mouth for keeps. And with her dead — "

"Do they need to know she is dead?"

"Well, that's an angle, Bates!" The postmaster's gaunt, homely face lightened. Then suddenly it soured. "But what about this nurse that John Walker went to town for? If she comes in and finds her dead, the word will go around."

"She won't get in this room, Tobacco."

16

LAMPLIGHT glistened in the hallway. Judge Bates, his broad back to the door, looked at the plump nurse, who had gasped with surprise.

"Well, I never — Here I come all this way to nurse Miss Helper and you, Judge Bates, want to send me back to Muletown! Why did you send for me in the first place if you don't want me to see the patient?"

Tobacco Jones, slumped in a chair, regarded Bart Terry and John Walker with speculative eyes, all the time listening to the nurse's angry words. Terry and Walker did not see his calculated study, though; their backs were toward him as they, along with the nurse, looked at Judge Bates.

The sudden death of Ree Helper had put the judge and Tobacco Jones in a rather difficult spot. They had to keep Terry and Walker from knowing of the girl's demise. And to do so they had to keep the nurse from entering the bedroom wherein lay the girl's corpse.

"What's the idea?" Walker demanded. "You sent me into town for this nurse. When I come out with her you won't let her in the room. I don't savvy it, Judge Bates."

"What's the play?" Bart Terry demanded.

"What is it to you two?" His Honor demanded. "You the girl's relatives or something? You sure seem worried over a woman who is supposed to have no blood ties to you two! What's the matter with you gents?"

Terry said, "Don't get rough with me, Bates. I own this ranch, remember? You're standing in a building owned by me, and don't forget it!"

"This building," His Honor said, "is under federal jurisdiction. I'm a federal judge, and to place this building in this classification I need only use my judicial powers."

"You can't — " Terry began, then suddenly stopped. For the moment anger had overruled logic, and Terry had been quick to let logic come to the surface. He glanced at John Walker, who said nothing, letting Terry carry the ball.

Judge Bates asked slowly, "I can't do *what*, Terry?"

Terry was instantly politic. "I shall cooperate with you all the way, Your Honor, and we shall comply with your wishes."

"Good," the judge said, presumably in a mellower mood. "Get your men off this ranch, Terry. I want nobody on this spread but the sick woman and Mr Jones and myself. All other persons can only enter the premises with my permission."

"Dictatorship," the nurse scoffed, her heavy breasts rising in anger. "Judge Bates, no wonder no woman ever married you — you're as stubborn as a jackass in a bog during bull-fly time! Why in the name of Christmas did you get me out all the distance from town, and then not even let me look at the patient?"

"The reason, madam, is simple."

"Simple, eh?" Two strong hands were planted on two broad hips in belligerent stance. "What's so simple about a woman bouncing along in a buckboard, her kidneys getting wrapped around her lungs with such a bumpy road — "

Judge Bates interrupted rudely with, "Don't go theatrical on me, young lady. Life has enough complications without you adding more. You should be on the stage — a Concord stage."

"Such humour!" scoffingly.

The judge said quietly, "If you get off the platform for a while, I'll tell you why there is no use in seeing Miss Helper. I thought you could set a bone. Her arm is broken. You just admitted you could not set a bone. Miss Helper is resting comfortably. When you get in town, send a telegram to Laramie, and get a doctor out from there. There is no need to set a bone immediately after fracture. A few days can elapse safely before the bone is set. Is that not correct, young lady?"

"That's correct."

Judge Bates spoke to John Walker. "I'd appreciate it, sir, if you would take this lady back to town. And stay off this ranch, too. And that goes for you, too, Mr. Terry."

Walker's face, for a moment, showed a rise of resentment, but Terry, as usual, was complying, apparently bending himself to Judge Bates' orders.

"Okay," Walker grunted.

Terry said smoothly, quietly, "I'd like to go in and wish Miss Helper a speedy recovery, Your Honor. After all, she is my neighbor, you know."

"Nobody sees her, Terry."

"Why not?"

Judge Bates played his top ace. He did it smoothly and without effort, sliding it out into plain view.

"Miss Helper has something to tell me and Tobacco. Some secret information pointing to the reason why there is a fight over Thunder Canyon. She has promised to tell us what the fight is all about."

Walker stood silent, gaunt and ugly, the shadow of his form against the wall, and he was silent. Terry nodded, his eyes down for a moment, and when he lifted them they were clear.

The nurse, like Walker, said nothing.

"I would like to hear what she has to say," Bart Terry said slowly.

"It will be interesting," His Honor said. "So far, she has not talked, but she has given a promise that, if we summon a doctor, she will talk freely when the doctor comes, and we have agreed to this."

Terry said, "Fair enough. We should get this trouble settled for once and for all. If you send to Laramie, the doctor will get here within about forty-eight hours, or a little less. He will come in on the train day after tomorrow, Your Honor. That leaves you the rest of this night and tomorrow night, and then the doctor will get here. Again, her testimony will probably prove informative."

"It will point out a guilty person," His Honor said.

The nurse said, "I'm going out to the rig."

She stalked out, back stiff as a poker. She slammed the door hard. Walker followed her, but Terry remained a moment.

"I'll get my men off the ranch, sir."

Judge Bates said, "Yes, and take that guard away, too."

"Guard?"

"Don't play innocent, Terry. You got guards out. Get them away, or Jones and I will scout the brush and kill them."

"You sound tough, Bates."

"And we are tough," Tobacco Jones said roughly.

Terry whirled, looked at the postmaster, then said, "All right. Just you two alone on this ranch with Ree Helper. And I hope she tells you something, gentlemen. As a taxpayer and honest citizen — "

"The honest citizen," His Honor said, "always takes a beating, the poor fellow."

"Not to mention the taxpayer," Tobacco Jones said, and deliberately spat at Bart Terry's polished boots. He missed and said, "My aim is bad, Bates."

Terry's fists hardened, and he stood

there for a moment — etched against the lamplight, meticulously dressed, a domineering man used to bending people to his will and orders. But this was a pair he could not bend, and this fact made him angry for a moment, but that anger was short-lived.

"You two," he said, "are looking for trouble."

That logic dispensed, he stalked dawn the hall.

When he went out, though, he did not slam the door.

"He sure can control himself," Tobacco Jones said. "Tough man, Bates, and you, my friend, are a top liar of the first water."

"White lies," His Honor said.

"Think it will lure them in, Bates?"

"I hope so."

Tobacco Jones said, "I'd hate to git killed by either of them hellions, Bates. I'm still a young man with lots of good days ahead of me . . ." His smile was a little wistful, but the judge read purpose in it.

They went out on the porch. The Terry riders were saddling and getting ready to leave the ranch. The buckboard whirled past, wheels hammering dust upward, and the nurse, nose in the air, had no eyes for them. John Walker, tooling the lines, also apparently did not see the partners.

"Her nose is kinda high," Tobacco Jones said.

"So is his, Jones."

The buckboard went around the toe of the hill and became lost from view. The riders lifted themselves into their saddles and loped away, Bart Terry following. They rode out with jarring hoofs and Terry lifted his arm in salutation. Then the entire company was gone, the hill hiding them.

"And a dead woman inside," Tobacco Jones said solemnly.

"We got them scared," Judge Bates said.

Tobacco nodded, then bit off a fresh chew. He threw his old cud down into the dust and masticated the new tobacco thoroughly.

"They'll come back before that doctor gets here, Bates. I'm danged sure of that; I do wish we knew what was in their minds, though."

"So do I."

Terry beat Walker into town, for the rig slowed down Walker's advance. Walker drove the nurse to her home and she invited him in for coffee, but he turned her down, for a sour mood was on the gunman. He wheeled the rig to the livery stable and threw down the lines to the hostler with, "Unhook them and put them away, Slim."

"You sure lathered them up, Walker."

"A horse," said Walker, "takes the abuse of man. He's made for that. They even ride the innocent animal into bullets in so-called cavalry charges. And a horse gets shot down and killed and he hates nobody."

The hostler looked at him. "Since when did you become a philosopher, Walker?"

"The last few miles," Walker said, and went toward the saloon. When he passed the Broken Spur Café, Lou called to him and asked about Judge Bates. She seemed down-hearted because the judge was going to stay at the Terry ranch. Walker was again stopped before he reached Terry's saloon. This time he was hailed down by Imogene Carter, who also asked about His Honor.

"The judge seems popular," Walker said, showing his thin smile, his eyes on the attractive woman. "Is it his prestige or his salary that attracts you, Miss Carter?" He was caustically polite.

"You have a sharp tongue," she said sarcastically.

He bowed, making the bow a little too deep, and anger flushed her face, giving her character. Then he went through the saloon and entered Terry's office without knocking. Terry was seated in the far corner cleaning a Winchester .30–30 rifle, and he looked up with a slight frown.

Walker looked at the rifle. "Rifle work, you figure?"

"Both rifles and short-guns."

Walker said, "They're deadly with them scatterguns they pack. They got Spud and Killer right off with those shotguns. They pack pistols too. And a combination of short-guns and shotguns is hard to beat, Bart."

"Rifles and short-guns beat it," Terry said.

Walker settled in the big chair and spread out his legs and seemed to admire his boots. Terry slid the breech back and forth, testing the Winchester: the sound was metallic and sharp.

Finally Walker said, "When?"

Terry looked up, head canted. He seemed deep in thought. "The night has no moon," he said. "A man blunders in the dark, even if he knows his surroundings, and a blundering sound brings bullets. Dawn comes early, though."

"In the morning, eh?"

"Bright and early."

Walker said, "You left a guard, didn't you?"

"I did. I pulled him back, though. I know a little bit about military law. I spent a hitch in the army."

"In the guard-house?"

"In the hospital," Terry said, grinning. "beds are better than in the clink. They finally threw me out for a gold-bricker. But I did some reading while on my back, and when you make a military reservation you have an area a mile deep around the objective."

"You got the guard beyond that?"

"I have."

Walker stood up, lanky and serious, and he nodded and said, "Good deal." He stretched and went to the door. "I'm going upstairs and chin with the girls, Bart. You know where I'm at when you need me."

"I'll know," Terry said.

Walker closed the door slowly, and the last sound he heard from the office was the clicking of the .30–30's breech.

17

TOBACCO JONES said, "They still got a guard out. About a mile beyond the house, on a butte. Settin' there watchin' this spread, Bates."

"Where is he?"

Tobacco pointed at a dark rise of land to the north, a butte black with igneous rocks and the shadows of thick pine trees.

"How far away would you say that rise is, Tobacco?"

Tobacco Jones chewed, deliberated and said, "About a mile. No, over a mile, Bates. But what difference does that make — he's still a guard and he still watches us. And you told them to post no guards, remember?"

They were on the long porch of the Terry ranch-house. They had watered the livestock and had fed grain to the few chickens Terry maintained. Now, their chores done, they were loafing. Tobacco had ridden out on a scouting excursion right after watering the work-horses and had spotted the guard in the boulders.

"They weren't supposed to stake out a guard, Bates."

Judge Bates sat on the bench. He uncorked his jug and drank. The Wyoming dusk was very still, and the dead woman inside, lying on the big bed, was missing her first sunset, and this thought was with His Honor.

"Evidently one of them knows something about military law, Jones. Under military regulations one can post a guard within a mile of the object put under military rule. Probably one of them has been in the War, or else in the army."

"I don't remember them things in the War, Bates."

"You probably never had occasion to meet such a circumstance, Tobacco." The judge took another drink. "Hope my jug doesn't run dry . . . By the way, there's a stove in the kitchen, and lots of grub in the cupboard . . . Need more be said?"

"Sure," Tobacco Jones said sourly. "You do the cookin'!"

The judge whipped up a fast meal that consisted of scrambled eggs and toast and coffee. The long twilight lingered. The meal done, the partners leaned back, and the judge did some talking, with Tobacco asking occasional questions. Their problem settled, they saddled their broncs and rode away from the Terry spread, heading toward Muletown.

"The guard cain't help but see us, Bates."

"Just what we want."

They rode around the toe of the butte, and the rise of the land hid them from the guard. Also, the night was coming down fast, and darkness was a mantle of secrecy wrapped about their movements. They pulled in, and the judge said, "Now you head for Muletown. Make sure that either Walker or Terry sees you. Tell them I'm at the hotel, and we came in for whisky and tobacco, and that Ree

Helper is resting so nice we thought she did not need us."

Tobacco nodded, his long face hidden by the night.

"Give the impression we'll be gone until tomorrow forenoon."

"Thet guard will beat me into town, Bates."

"That's all right. Now I head back to the ranch."

"Good luck, Bates."

"Same to you, pard."

Tobacco spurred into the night. Slowly the judge rode back to the Terry ranch. He tied his bronc back in the brush where the animal would be hidden. Then, his pistol riding his hip, his shotgun in hand, he approached the house. He did not go inside. He hunkered beside the house, a dark shadow in the dark night, and he gave way to his thoughts. For some reason, he kept remembering the dead salesman: the man had joked and made fun, and he had been filled with life. But a bullet had snuffed that joviality short, and somewhere a widow and children mourned.

Time ran on, the night lengthened, and Judge Bates dozed. He came awake, and he realized a dream had awakened him — he had dreamed Tobacco was in danger. But this dream proved false. Tobacco Jones, upon reaching Muletown, had come into the livery barn by the rear door, and he had found the place deserted of human occupants. And he had wanted it this way.

He put his spent horse in a stall, gave him a brief pat of thanks, and threw his saddle on a big midnight black — a powerful horse that he guessed would have long endurance. He did not know who owned the bronc — he did not care. This done, he led the horse into the brush along Mule Creek, and tied him there. Then he went to the Terry saloon.

He came into the brightly lighted place and stood in the doorway deliberately, blinking his eyes against the brightness of the saloon. He saw a man move away from a far wall and go toward the door at the end of the building. Terry's watcher had spotted him immediately.

Tobacco went to the bar where he bought three plugs of Horseshoe. "And a glass of water, barkeeper."

"Water?"

"Yes, water. Some people even wash in it, remember?"

"First time for everything," the bartender said, and spun out a glass of water. "No pay, Jones. On the house."

"Thanks." Ironically.

Terry moved in close, said, "Something harder, Jones?"

"Never touch it, but thanks."

Terry lifted a little finger, and the barkeeper gave him a jigger and a bottle. Terry poured slowly and deliberately. His hand trembled slightly, though.

"Thought you and the judge were going to stay out at the ranch?"

Tobacco drank some of his water. Where was John Walker? Well, it made little 'count where Walker was: Bart Terry was the kingpin.

"The judge got a cramp in his belly.

He rode into town for some powders he had at the hotel. And me, I run out of eatin' terbaccer."

"The judge — he's at the hotel?"

"In our room, asleep. Powders quieted him down right pronto."

"What about Miss Helper? She out there — alone?"

"That guard you had posted might be with her now. He saw us leave but we never talked to him. We aim to head out in the mornin' right after we've et. She's well enough — o'nery as anything — keeps her mouth shut. Judge Bates an' me questioned her, but she sure is a tough one."

"Won't say a word, eh?"

"Cain't get a word out of her. Well, I gotta git to my hotel room an' git some shut-eye. You boys wired for that doc, I suppose?"

"We sent a wire," Bart Terry lied.

Tobacco paid and left. He went into the hotel by the front door, went up the stairs after deliberately nodding to the clerk, and even banged the door on an empty room, to give the impression he had gone into their room. This ruse accomplished, he went down the back stairway, followed the alley out of town, and within a few moments, was riding hard toward the Terry ranch, grinning from ear to ear.

Sure fooled Terry, he thought.

He pushed through a night as black as the inside of an old hat, following the trail more by instinct than by eyesight. The black horse was willing and seemed to know the trail, a fact which for a time puzzled the lanky postmaster, who rode high on his stirrups, looking much like Ichabod Crane, his elbows crooked and the wind whipping back his shirt. His right hand went down and felt along the sweaty shoulder of the gelding, and his fingers traced there the scarred outlines of the bronc's brand. And when he straightened again in leather, his smile was wide and happy. The bronc packed the Terry iron. He had stolen — no, *borrowed* — one of Terry's top horses. He had added insult to injury. He had heaped the burning coals higher on the pride of one Bart Terry.

Bates would grin when he heard this news.

With this merriment, though, was a sort of grim tragedy, for unless he was wrong, the dawn would see the smash and roll of gunfire, and somebody would die. Of course, the element of surprise would be on his side and the side of Judge Lemanuel Bates. This held some comfort, but the thought of death was always close, for this range was a range of death. But what the gods knew, they kept from revealing; when the time came, the truth would come out . . . and only when the correct moment arrived.

He did not ride openly to the big ranch. And as he drew closer to the Terry spread, he checked the gait of his black, until finally the animal hit a plodding gait. And the black welcomed this slow plod, for the night's run had beaten the energy out of him, putting gray lather across his black shoulders. They came to a point behind the house, and there in the willows the postmaster dismounted and tied the black to a cottonwood, hoping that the animal was securely hidden. Then, he worked his way toward the house, and once he glanced back — his horse was hidden by willows and the night.

Judge Bates had told him, before he had left for Muletown, where he would be hidden, and the postmaster stopped and looked at this point against the foundation of the house, and he could see no darkness saying that his partner hunkered there. For a moment fear ripped across him, talons digging into him. He went over possible points: had the guard come to the house and fought it out and killed Judge Bates? No, the guard had been in town when he left, for the guard had ridden in to report to Bart Terry and John Walker.

"Friend," he called.

"This way, friend."

The words came from his left and they turned him quickly, his shotgun rising slightly before memory rushed in and identified the speaker. Soon he hunkered beside his partner and he disclosed his mission's success, even to minute details. And Judge Bates nodded.

"Will they hit tonight, Bates?"

"I doubt it. They think we are at the hotel. You did a good job. But they might hit, at that."

Tobacco said, "Dawn is almost here. Gets daylight about three-thirty here during this time of the year, and at this high altitude. Dang, but that night air is chilly, comin' down from them snowy peaks."

"Trout like cold water."

"Why talk about trout at a time like this — with a dead woman inside this house, with two killers ridin' out, with dead men across this range? Bates, why talk about trout?"

"Mule Creek."

"What about Mule Creek?"

"We came to fish it, remember."

They hunkered there. A rooster crowed, and the hens came out of the henhouse and started to scratch in the dust. A horse

247

stamped at the barn, evidently wanting to get out into the rising sun, out on green pasture. Tobacco got to his feet, shotgun under his arm.

"Wonder if that guard is watching us?"

"No, he isn't, Jones."

Tobacco studied the judge's wide face. "And what makes you so certain, prophet Bates?"

Judge Bates stood up, too, and grimaced, his lips twisted in pain. "Got a leg cramp, Jones. The jurist is getting old . . . Hades, man, they'll keep that guard in town. They'll ride to do murder, and murder wants no eyes to watch its dastardly cowardice. Or so it seems to this man."

Tobacco said, "And to me too, Bates. Well, pard, good shooting, and shoot to kill. They're ruthless."

Judge Bates nodded.

Their plan of action had been discussed at great length, and now the time had come to move to stations and await the next turn of events. They did not shake hands. Both understood the other; no hand grip was necessary.

They had shared the same blankets, eaten from the same dutch-oven, and they had known each other for years.

"Good luck, Tobacco."

"The same to you and more of it, Bates."

Turning, Judge Lemanuel Bates went to the rear of the ranch house. There he placed a ladder against the eave and lifted his weight to the roof, carrying his shotgun and his jug of whiskey. Once on the roof, he pushed the ladder back, letting it topple to the ground. Had a pair of field glasses looked this house over they might have discerned the ladder and suspicion might have come into the eyes of the man behind the field glasses.

The judge climbed the roof, having a somewhat difficult time handling both his jug and the scattergun, for the steep incline made walking difficult — his boots threatened to slip on the shingles. But he reached the ridge-beam and climbed over it, almost sliding down the far side of the roof. With difficulty, he went down slowly, and then he was behind the chimney, hidden from anybody who might happen to ride into the yard, hidden from any possible viewers who would get the rear of the ranch-house in their field glasses.

Carefully he braced his jug against the rock chimney. Then he settled down, boots braced against the chimney, his jug between his boots, his shotgun barrel down, also against the chimney to keep it from sliding off the roof. Thus settled, the yard below him clearly in view when he glanced around the chimney, Judge Lemanuel Bates gave his attention to the windmill, which was across the yard about fifty or sixty feet distant.

Like all windmills, it had a ladder bolted to it, for the fan had to be greased. Made of logs, one bolted to the other, the windmill was a sturdy affair about forty feet in height. But His Honor was not interested in the windmill as such; his interest lay in Tobacco Jones, who had climbed the wooden ladder and right now was in the act of climbing over the top platform.

The postmaster got onto the platform with some difficulty, for he also had his sawed-off shotgun. First, he put the gun on the platform, and then his long legs came up, and he stood on the raised portion. Judge Bates saw him test it for strength, jumping up and down. Evidently the platform was strong enough, for the postmaster hunkered down, back to an upright timber, his shotgun across his knees. And the yard, too, was visible to him.

Tobacco glanced at Judge Bates, saw him and lifted his hand slightly. And the judge, always cautious and wary, considered their positions. He was safe, for the fireplace hid him. Tobacco, too, was hidden. He had height, for one thing, and then, too, the platform was big, running all around the top of the windmill tower. This hid Tobacco. Also, who looks up in the air at a windmill tower when he rides into a ranch-house yard?

These things clear in his mind, His Honor waited, impatience becoming raw and eager inside of him. Across the distance Tobacco Jones hunkered on the platform, a compact ball of humanity, his shotgun beside him. His Honor looked across the clean sweep of the Wyoming high country with its pine and grass and rising mountains, and he marveled momentarily at the ignorance and greed of Man.

Time seemed to drag by on slow hoofs, and again he remembered the genial salesman, Henry Moore. He pushed this memory out of his mind, but still it lurked on the rim of his memory. Simple, good-natured. He would sell no more liniment. He had died that a man named Judge Lemanuel Bates might live . . .

Within ten minutes, they rode into the yard.

They were killers and they came to murder a woman, and they did not know that that woman was already dead, her lips and mind sealed for eternity. They rode with a proud arrogance, killers both, and they rode openly into the yard, for they owned this spread — and did not Judge Bates and Tobacco Jones sleep in the hotel? Had they not tested the door and found it locked?

They came into the yard with their horses at a running walk, that fast pace a cow pony uses, halfway between a trot and a fast walk. And beneath the hoofs of their ponies lifted the endless and gray dust of old Wyoming. There was nothing to fear, for this ranch was deserted. Even the guard had left the country — he had received his pay and had ridden north toward Montana. They would kill this woman and bury her in the badlands, and when Judge Bates and Tobacco Jones arrived they would believe that the woman had strayed in delirium and her body would never be found. A person did that — a delirious person. He was apt to get out of bed and walk, and who could know what had happened — if the body was never found?

This was their plan, and they had

talked it over in Terry's office, and now they were out to execute it. They'd walk into the house, rifles in hand. Maybe it would be best not to shoot her in the house, for the bullets would leave holes in the bed and the walls and floors. No, they'd drag her outside, and kill her somewhere back in the brush, and then the badlands would receive her grave. This was their plan and they rode in and dismounted, pulling rifles from saddle-holsters.

They said not a word, and danger was thick on their shoulders.

Judge Bates had seen them, and his throat tightened — He had glanced at Tobacco Jones, squatted there like a buzzard on that platform; the postmaster had seen them too, and he had been watching their advance. Now two saddled horses, saddles empty, stood below them; two killers, toting rifles, were moving toward the front door, boots scuffling dust.

And then, from his high perch, Judge Bates said, "Nobody is going into this house, savvy. You two fell for our trap and — "

"What the blazes, Bart?"

The squeal had come from John Walker. A squeal of rage, of surprise. They both stopped as though they had run into a high, thick stone wall. They stood there, staring upward at Judge Bates, and the rising sun glistened on their eyes.

Bart Terry's voice was a startled croak. "Judge Bates!"

"And Tobacco Jones," the postmaster said, his voice as weird as that of Terry.

John Walker wheeled, glaring upward at the windmill. But Bart Terry did not turn, for Terry had himself under control now — he was all steel, all power, all killer. And his eyes were on Judge Lemanuel Bates' shotgun.

"Where is Jones, Walker?"

"Up on the platform — the windmill — "

Terry nodded, his eyes still on Judge Bates. Terry said, "They've got their shotguns and we got rifles. Spread out, John, and you take Jones, and Bates is my

255

meat. All right, Bates, this is it — "

Walker hollered, "Give them the works, Bart — "

And then the guns roared.

The gunfight happened with terrible suddenness, for although the judge and Tobacco Jones had been ready, the two killers went into action with erratic swiftness. Judge Bates had expected Terry to swing his rifle up, his thumb dropping the hammer. But Terry did not use his rifle.

Neither, for that matter, did Walker use his Winchester.

Terry was a cat, leaping to one side — a giant of a cat, balanced and graceful. And as he leaped he dropped his Winchester. Evidently he figured it to be too cumbersome; he figured it would take too much time to raise it, to level it, to fire. So Terry dropped the .30–30 and grabbed his six-shooter.

Walker did the same.

When the judge saw the Winchester twinkle in the sun, he shot at it, intending to knock the gun down, to get at the man behind the .30–30. But Terry only dropped the gun and the judge's beebees knocked it kicking, with only a few stinging Bart Terry. And Terry's .45 reared upward, winking hotly.

Momentary fear was a fiery jet of flame through the jurist. By a neat measure, executed with lightning swiftness, Terry had outguessed him — just as John Walker had also bested Tobacco Jones.

Terry was on one knee, a ball of hate, and out of this ball came gunfire. Afterwards, Judge Bates remembered a bullet slamming into a rock in the chimney so close the richochet sounded like a roar. But Terry shot too fast, and in his haste he lacked accuracy, and the judge fired his remaining barrel.

He fired down on Terry, and he hit him solidly. He drove the man down to the ground, making him drop his pistol. Terry rolled over once, then sat up, and he held his belly. He made no move for his six-shooter lying ten feet away in the dust.

By now, Judge Bates had his own short-gun pulled, but he did not use it. He slowly lowered the hammer, looking down at John Walker who lay on his belly, one arm outflung, his pistol lying a little beyond his open fingers. Then His Honor looked up at Tobacco Jones.

"Are you all right, pard?"

"One came so close it singed my whiskers. Walker should be dead, the rat — I got him in the face. You go down, Bates, while I hold a bead on Terry."

Sick at heart, his belly tight and tense, Judge Bates slid off the roof, dropping about eight feet to the ground, pistol in hand. He bent to his knees as he dropped, and he broke his fall this way, coming upright with his pistol on Terry, who had got to his feet.

"Watch yourself, Terry."

Terry said nothing. His mouth twisted, he held his hands over his belly, and he walked toward the front door — a puppet pulled by unseen strings, a dead man walking with stiff knees.

Judge Bates watched him, and from the corner of one eye, he saw Tobacco Jones scrambling down the ladder, moving with the swiftness of a scared monkey. Then His Honor put his gaze back on Bart Terry.

His legs rigid pokers, Terry was crossing the porch, still holding his belly. And His Honor followed, wondering at the man's purpose, surprised by his strength. Apparently Terry did not notice him. If he did, he paid the judge no attention. They went into the house, with Judge Bates trailing in amazement.

Terry crossed the living room, went into the hall. He went toward the bedroom holding the body of Ree Helper. He was a wolf, wounded and dying, and he was returning to his den, dragging his broken body.

Only sheer will power kept him on his feet.

He turned the corner, and then he was in the bedroom. He stood there, looking down at Ree Helper, and he put both hands over his belly. He looked at the woman and then he looked at Judge Bates.

"You've killed me, Bates."

Judge Bates said nothing. He couldn't speak. The man's eyes glowed, hate was there, but fear was greater than hate — fear of death.

Terry looked back at Ree Helper.

He said slowly, "I loved her — the only woman I ever loved."

His knees failed. He went to his knees beside the bed.

Judge Bates watched, heartsick.

Bart Terry moved his head forward slowly, and then his lips found the cold lips of Ree Helper. He kissed her, and then his hand came up — a bloody broken hand — and it touched Ree Helper's throat.

"Bates, you lied. She's dead."

Again, His Honor said nothing.

Terry said, "I got blood on her throat." He kissed her again, the effort costing him pain, energy. Then he looked at Judge Bates, and his voice was a low croaking sound. "You'd like to know about Thunder Canyon?"

"Yes."

"You'll never find out from me." He looked again at the dead woman. "I came to kill her, and I stayed to love her and die beside her. Ree, honey, hold me tight, like you held me that night in the alley, for I'm coming with you, Ree. Hold me, honey, while I die — "

His head went down beside hers on the pillow.

Judge Bates walked outside. Tobacco Jones came to him, face pale from the stress, the terror.

"Walker can tell nothing. He's dead, Bates."

"We know nothing more then, for Terry died kissing Ree Helper."

They looked at each other. Tragedy held them in its grip, and both hated themselves for what they had been forced to do.

"We still don't know," Tobacco said.

Judge Bates said, "We'd best get to Muletown and get out help."

They went for their broncs.

18

LOU said, "Gee, Judge, haven't I got a pretty face, or are you blind?"

The judge whipped out his trout line. "You sure have, girl." He gave her a moment's glance. She had made no understatement. She stood in clear water to her knees, her levis rolled up. And she was smiling and happy, her eyes glowing.

"Do you like my looks, Lem?"

"I sure do, Lou."

She pouted. "You're more interested in that old fish line!"

The judge cast again. He pulled a brook trout out from under an overhanging rock. He handed the wriggling fish to Lou, who put it in the creel she carried.

"Gee, cast over that way. Under those fern pads."

The judge's line whipped out, the fly

hit the surface of Mule Creek, but no trout lunged upward.

Lou said, "Almost two weeks since you and Tobacco had the fight, Judge. Well, we found out about the copper and the railroad — but shucks, who killed Judge Weakspoon, and who killed Kirby Helper — "

"Hush, honey, let's forget, please."

The days had been busy ones for His Honor and Tobacco Jones. Inquests, investigations, and finally Tobacco had handed the star back to Engstrand, who had almost got down on his knees in thanks. From the railroad headquarters they had found out about the copper ledge and the railroad.

The rest did not matter. Dead men — and a dead woman — slept the eternal sleep.

Lou waded close to him. "I'm kinda pretty all the way around, ain't I, Lem?"

"You sure are."

She frowned, said, "You haven't kissed me yet, Lem. What's the matter with you? Are you sick?"

"No — smart."

"Why do you say that?"

"If I kissed you, I might get ideas about getting married, and I don't want to get married right now."

"Neither do I. I like my freedom too much."

Judge Bates smiled, a boyish smile. "That being the case, you should have told me before. Sister, you're going to get kissed!"

After they broke, Lou said, "Gee, I liked that, Judge. Wonder what Imogene and Tobacco are doing around the bend? Kiss me again, eh?"

At that particular moment Tobacco Jones had just snagged a big rainbow trout. Levis also rolled up, Imogene Carter was helping him land the fish, and she was, in reality, more of a hindrance than a help. But she saw to it she got her hands over his on the pole.

Finally they had the fish on the bank. He lay on the rushes, gills falling and rising, tail lifting.

"Eight pounds," Tobacco said. "Bates'll

never catch one that big."

Imogene pouted. "Why think of the judge at this moment? I helped you land that trout."

Tobacco didn't look up. He had expected this for some time. His eyes landed on her knees. She noticed this.

"Haven't I pretty knees, Tobacco?"

"You sure have, Imogene."

She turned around, letting him look her over. She filled her levis very prettily. The blue chambray shirt became her, too. She stopped in front of him.

"Kiss me."

"Why?"

"Because I like you. You like me. Kiss me?"

"I don't want to kiss you. I might fall in love with you and — shucks, I don't wanna get married."

She smiled. "Neither do I. I been married and divorced. No more double-harness for Imogene. Now do we understand each other?"

"We sure do, honey."

"First, there's one thing, though."

She was in his arms. The trout flapped, then settled down. She was lovely and fresh and young.

"What is that?"

"Before you kiss me you have to throw away that chew of tobacco."

Tobacco Jones grinned. "Fooled you. Ain't chewin' tobacco. Gum!" He held it out on his tongue.

She kissed him. Finally they broke, and Tobacco yelled, "Hey, Bates."

Through the buckbrush came, "Over here. What is it?"

"I just caught an eight pounder, if he weighs an ounce. Bet you ain't got one that big yet."

The judge had both arms around Lou. "I sure have. Got one that weighs at least one hundred and fifteen pounds."

Lou acted hurt. "That wasn't a bit nice, Judge Bates. I'm no fish and I want you — " She didn't finish.

The judge saw to that with a grin.